JOHN MCLAUGHLIN

OUR TIME IN THE SUN

A Novel

Cold Tree Press
Nashville, Tennessee

Library of Congress Control Number: 2007938696

Published by Cold Tree Press
Nashville, Tennessee
www.coldtreepress.com

Printed in the United States of America
978-1-58385-239-2

*"People sleep peaceably
in their beds
at night only because
rough men stand ready
to do violence on their behalf."*

—GEORGE ORWELL

Dedicated to
Law Enforcement Officers in Arizona:
Past, Present, and Future

In memory of my dad
He would've made one heck of a Ranger
&
For these with love
My wife and best good friend, Sylvia
& my boys, Chris and Jonathan

with special thanks to
Heidi Thomas, Editor

AUTHOR'S NOTE

The story of the Arizona Rangers deserves to be revisited for its legendary, intriguing tales of shootouts and long, hard days in the saddle battling the criminal element at the turn of the century. Equally important to me is unveiling the personalities of this small band of lawmen who dedicated themselves to protect the citizens of the Territory of Arizona at a time in history that was rife with violence and lawlessness. Who were these lawmen? Where did they come from and what were their personal lives like at this critical juncture in Arizona history?

The Arizona Territory, a haven for rustlers, bandits, train robbers, and outlaws who operated with impunity, desperately sought the establishment of law and order, especially along the Mexican border. It was here that murder, rustling, and train robberies were commonplace events that continued unabated and an atmosphere of violence existed.

The Arizona Rangers were created in 1901 by the territorial legislature to bring the situation under control. My Dad lived in Arizona shortly after the political demise of the Arizona Rangers, and he spoke fondly of this legendary band of men. *The Arizona Rangers* by Bill O'Neal is the first documented history of the Rangers ever published and provides accurate historical information. My intention has always been to write a *fictional* story about the Arizona Rangers depicting the personalities of historical and fictional characters involved in real life issues of the times while maintaining a tale based on fact, true to the times.

I have spent over twenty years as a Law Enforcement

Ranger living in Arizona and working for the National Park Service and the Bureau of Land Management, patrolling by truck, riding horse back, packing mules, and camping often in areas that were frequented by the old Rangers.

I have sat out in the Arizona desert many a dark, cold night waiting for the bad guys to show on drug-related details near the border. I thought a lot about the old Rangers, wondering how it must have been for them as lawmen. Their voices whispered softly out of the shadows and darkness to me as I sat quietly in the desert. And this is their story in a time long, long ago.

John D. McLaughlin

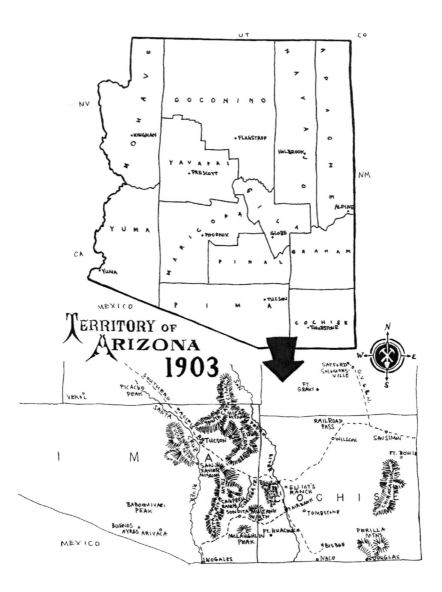

OUR TIME IN THE SUN

CHAPTER ONE
Arizona Territory, 1903

lliott crawled through the underbrush and sandy soil, his 1895 Winchester .30-.40 rifle cradled in his arms. A coral dawn began to usher in a clear blue sky. Birds chirped among the rocks and oak shrub trees, signaling another fine day in the Chiricahua Mountains of south-eastern Arizona Territory. He came up behind and to the right of a cottonwood tree with the new Ranger Frank Shaw right behind him, inching to a position to the left of the giant tree. Elliott suppressed a sudden desire to sneeze from the strong pungent odor of rabbit brush on his face and clothes.

About a hundred yards distant in a clearing intermingled with oak trees and bear grass, the outlaws moved slowly about their camp. One man walked a short distance from camp and began to relieve himself while another placed a coffee pot on the campfire.

Elliott scanned the camp. *Where the hell's Chacon? Thet thievin', murderin'* .... His eyes hardened, jaws clenched tight. He had tracked the wily outlaw many times in the past only to have him slip away. Rancher Bob Williams and his cowpuncher were the latest in the infamous bandit's string of crimes. Witnesses had confirmed it was Chacon and his band who had brutally murdered the two men. Then Chacon had stolen 150 head of cattle from the dead man.

Carlos Ayala's clear authoritative voice rang out in the still morning air, "Arizona Rangers! We got you surrounded ... git your hands in the air! All of yah, *now!*"

Surprised, the outlaws hesitated. Ayala, the only Mexican Ranger in the company, repeated the command in Spanish and again quickly in English. The outlaws dropped to the ground, looking around in confusion.

Then Elliott spotted their leader, a dark-complected man wearing a large, black sombrero and dark clothing. The outlaw leader glanced in the direction the commands came from, then reached for a rifle leaning against a tree and crouched down behind it. Chacon yelled back across the creek, "What do you want *amigos*? We haf done nothin' wrong. *¿Que quieren?*

"You're all under arrest!" Ayala boomed out, "Git your hands up, no guns, and come out! *¡'horita!*

Elliott cocked the hammer of his loaded rifle, looked through the adjustable sights, and drew a bead on the outlaw who had been relieving himself. *I shore hope he wet hisself.* The bandit clutched his rifle and swung it from one point to another, finally toward the Rangers' positions in the rocky outcropping. Elliott only hoped that Shaw was sighted in on another outlaw from the other side of the old tree. A young man, Shaw had arrived in Arizona from Kansas prior to enlisting in the Arizona Rangers. *How in the hell do I always end up volunteerin' to take the new feller with me? Wel-l-l ...* One thing was certain; the outlaws wouldn't be making their escape past his location west of their encampment.

Then Chacon did a strange thing. He stood up and walked out into the clearing, dragging his rifle behind him with his right hand and waving with his left hand. He spoke slowly, scouring the vegetation. *"Amigos,* ees Señor Elliott with jew? *¿Donde esta?"* He paused as if waiting for an answer, and receiving none, continued, "We mean yew no harm. Show us that yew weel not shoot us, *amigos.*Come out here weeth me and we weel talk."

He spat tobacco juice, a residual dribbling down his unshaven chin. "You keep that Elliott son-of-a-beech— away from us. I know what he deed to them indeens years ago. I weel talk man to man weeth any other Ranger. Come to me ... we talk."

Elliott gritted his teeth. *Yeah, we'll talk—ya yeller bastard— with the business end o' this here rifle.* His sudden surge of hatred turned to dismay as Carlos Ayala stepped out from cover and approached Chacon in the open.

From twenty feet away, Ayala barked, "Git your hands up!" He motioned to the other outlaws, "You other men, come on out with your hands up and surrender." Elliott swung his rifle over to look through his rifle sights directly at Chacon. *No ...Carlos, no ...git back, dammit!* Suddenly, in Elliott's peripheral vision he saw the outlaw who had urinated earlier bring his rifle up to point it up toward Ayala.

As Elliott swung his rifle back on that outlaw, Chacon dropped to one knee, brought his rifle up with his right hand and shot Ayala. Ayala groaned, dropped his rifle, clutched his belly, and crumpled to the ground.

Elliott's rifle belched flame and the first outlaw fell to the ground shot through the head. He heard Shaw firing and swung his weapon back to where Chacon had been. The outlaw had disappeared. Elliott heard the report of Chapo Carter's Mauser and Harry Wheeler's Winchester from the rocky ridge coupled with the screams of men hit hard.

Sergeant Wheeler took charge from behind cover. "Cease fire! Cease fire! You men throw your guns down, get your hands up, and come out—*Now!*"

Gunsmoke filled the cool morning air. Ayala had not moved from where he had fallen. Elliott drew his revolver. "Shaw! Cover me! I'm goin' fer Carlos." Not waiting for an answer, he arose and ran straight toward Ayala. A sharp pain stabbed through his right knee. *Dammit ...not now!* He stumbled, lost his balance and fell hard, rolled, got up, and ran hard with gritted teeth. Sliding in next to Ayala, he heard bullets zing over his head and slam into the ground near him. *It's hell gittin' older in a young man's game.*

Simultaneously, Wheeler and Carter resumed firing into the outlaws' encampment. Elliott heard Shaw's rifle crack from behind and a man scream in agony. Ayala was doubled up on the ground in a fetal position, clutching his stomach with blood seeping out over his hands onto the ground.

"Carlos, *amigo*—can you make it back to cover with me?"

Ayala groaned. "I'm gut shot ... bad ... can't feel my legs." His face ashen, he grimaced in pain.

"Hang on, Carlos. We'll get ya outta here." Elliott touched the Ranger's shoulder. There was only one thing to do. If he stayed much longer, they'd both be killed. Using the cover of gun smoke in the air and whatever cover he could find, he raised his .45 revolver, and charged the outlaws, yelling at the other Rangers to move in.

As he sprinted forward, he saw three men lying on the ground; one moved toward his gun. Elliott shot him once in the face. He then turned to the other two prone bodies and shot each one in the head. *Damn your murderin' hides, I'll kill ever' damned one o' ya.* He gripped the .45 in his strong hand, supported by his weak hand, and brought it up to eye level. Off to his right, he heard a loud report and felt something pass through his jacket, tugging hard at the fabric. Turning his head and body together in one motion, his revolver fired twice in rapid succession at the man holding the gun that had just fired at him. The man tumbled backwards as the heavy .45 slugs tore through his chest.

Elliott knelt on one knee behind the cover of a tree, surveying the scene in front of him, his revolver still at eye level. He heard someone run up from behind and swung the revolver around to see Frank Shaw slide in behind a tree adjacent to him. "Jesus, Elliott! These four men are dead! Christ almighty!" The young Ranger's shock etched his pale face.

"Plumb dead fer shore," whispered Elliott. "Two others still on the loose, I reckon."

Wheeler skidded into position behind the tree with Elliott. "Where are the others?" he gasped.

Elliott turned to his boss, "It 'pears as if they was high-tailin' east outta here. Them rustled cows was penned up o'er yonder yesterdee when I scouted out the place. Maybe they got their hosses there as well."

"You alright with trailing them for a ways by yourself?" asked Wheeler. "I need these two other boys to help me with Ayala and to secure the scene."

"Yessir, I reckon so." Elliott looked to the east and quickly reloaded his revolver. Then he checked the other revolver in the shoulder holster beneath his left arm.

Wheeler sighed deeply and looked over at Shaw and Carter while addressing Elliott. "We'll get Carlos to the nearest ranch for help. If you find the others and need help, fire three times in the air, and we'll come running. I don't want you going too far after them. But we've got a wounded Ranger who will need all of us if he's going to make it."

Elliott nodded. *I reckon I'll hafta kill 'em ... fer what they done, by Gawd. And I ain't wastin' ammo.* He didn't particularly like following tracks without someone to watch his back, but he had done just that many times in the past. *You ought not jest be killin' ... ya promised.* His hate-filled, trained eyes picked up sign of overturned rocks, vegetation disturbed, broken branches. Moving slowly away from Wheeler, he kept his revolver in the ready position, focusing only on the dangerous job given to him.

Wheeler returned to Carlos Ayala still lying in a fetal position. Chapo Carter set down his Spanish Mauser rifle, knelt down and removed the Ranger's shirt and jacket to check for wounds. "He's hurt bad, Jefe. An entry wound in front above his belt buckle and a bigger exit wound out the back thet hit his spine." He swallowed hard and looked down at his friend, who was moaning. *Gut shot. My Gawd, what will Marie and the girls do now?*

"Tear up his shirt, pack and bind both wounds securely Chapo. If we need more bandage material, we'll take from the dead." While Carter followed instructions, Wheeler knelt down near Ayala's bloodless face. Shock was setting in. He truly began to doubt that the man could be saved.

"Carlos, can you hear me?"

"I ... can ... hear ... you," Ayala gasped. He writhed in agony. But he reached a shaking, bloody hand into his pants pocket, and with great difficulty he withdrew a silver dollar. "Give ... to ... my wife, *amigo*. ... all she'll be gettin'... from me ... now." He paused, gathering his last bit of strength, "... that an' ... maybe a month's pay. You tell her ... I love her!"

Wheeler patted his shoulder reassuringly. "You bet *amigo*! I give you my word, but we're going to get you out of this. You just hang on! Don't give up!"

He stood up and turned to Frank Shaw. "Check the dead men for identification and get all the firearms. Look for anything to help build a travois for Carlos. Hustle now!"

"What about the dead outlaws? You want me to bury them?"

Wheeler paused before replying, "Let the coyotes have 'em. We help our own first."

CHAPTER TWO

After tracking the two men from the outlaw encampment for about a half hour, Elliott hesitated behind the cover of a large oak tree. The outlaws had headed in an easterly direction on foot, running at first then walking. One man had been hurt in the firefight with the Rangers, evidenced by a sporadic trail of blood. Elliott carefully surveyed the scene in front of him. Clear tracks in the sand led into a side arroyo approximately fifty yards distant. The canyon narrowed at the entrance and then progressively opened at the other end. It offered plenty of cover and concealment on the far side, an excellent location for an ambush.

Elliott debated for just a moment the possibility of ambush against the urgency to return and help his fellow Rangers. His gut feeling from experience told him that most likely the injured outlaw had been left behind by Chacon to kill whoever had been sent to track them down. He made his decision, erring toward safety and circled south around the arroyo.

It took a good half hour to complete his flanking movement, occasionally crawling and stopping to listen. Finally, as he approached the east end of the arroyo from the backside, he detected a slight movement behind a boulder about fifty yards away. Elliott peered at the boulder, discerning colors and shape that were not consistent with the surrounding countryside and terrain. A man leaned against the rock with his revolver drawn and pointed toward the entrance to the arroyo. His left shoulder and arm hung useless, bloody.

Elliott cocked his revolver, and aimed at the outlaw. "¡*No se mueva! ¡Manos arriba!*"

The man jerked his head in Elliott's direction. Elliott yelled, "¡*Suelte la pistola! ¡Suéltela!* Drop it!"

Instead of putting his hands up, the outlaw dropped his right arm beside his leg, still holding the revolver.

"*Hombre* ... you haf me ... in a bad way. I am ... almost bled out ... now." The man leaned back against the boulder for support, exhaled and dropped his head. "I am very week—y *cansado*. Indio has gotten to the horses by now, *hombre* ... and he ees riding away to Mexico. I theenk ... I deed my job." He slumped to a sitting position against the boulder.

Elliott remained behind cover and kept his revolver aimed on the outlaw's chest. He again commanded that the man throw away the gun.

The outlaw listened intently. "Are you *Señor* Elliott?" Getting no reply, he continued, "*Indio dijo que* ... it would be you tracking us, *hombre*." He swallowed hard then took a deep breath. "He say ... you keel us, scalp us, and cut off our ears, hands ... our *huevos* like the *indios*. He say you—*muy malo hombre. Hombre* ... you come here. ¿*Porque no?*"

Burning sweat trickled down Elliott's face into his eyes and down his neck. *Easy now, no call to rush in an' get your damn fool head blowed off.* He was thirsty and his right knee throbbed from the exertion, but he still had the advantage of being behind cover with the outlaw in full view. He would have preferred to have his rifle or be closer to the outlaw. *I reckon ya ... most always end up playin' the hand given ya in life.*

Scalps? Yeah, he'd taken scalps. A red haze obscured his vision as he tightened his finger against the trigger.

A voice cut through the haze. "Hey *hombre. Venga aqui.* I theenk I am dying, *hombre.*

Elliott pushed the memories—the living nightmares—away as he had for so many years. Not now. *Por favor, Dios.*

Elliott had been a young, naïve man that terrible summer in 1870. *The filthy, murderin' savages.* He carefully placed the Henry rifle against a pine tree, steadying himself, and squeezed the trigger. The recoil of the rifle surprised him as the well placed round entered the Indian's head above the right ear and exited the left side, spraying bone fragments, blood and gray matter into the air. Elliott vaulted into the saddle and charged the other warriors.

A second Apache warrior hurriedly took aim at Elliott with his bow and arrow. He got off a quick shot that did not find its mark, and Elliott ran him down with his horse, trampling the Indian. Elliott turned in the saddle and shot him in the chest. Another warrior yelled and ran hard at Elliott, leaping in the air, shrieking; knocking him off his horse to the ground. They hit hard and rolled together several times clutched in a death grip. Elliott lost his rifle. The blade hit his ribs; a hot sharp bite first and then the blade raked several ribs. He gasped for air—there seemed to be none, and his strength that had been endless before was ebbing away. In desperation, he rolled to his right, finally got a good grip on the Indian's wrist with both hands and drove the Indian's hand, palm up, with all the force he could muster sharply back toward the warrior's shoulder. The Indian yelped and dropped the knife. Elliott hit him hard with the heel of his left hand, palm open, in the mouth and nose snapping the Indian's head back sharply. With all the strength he could muster, he swung his right fist hard into the Indian's throat, crushing his larynx.

The fourth Apache warrior had mounted his horse and charged. Elliott reached for his revolver. The Indian shot twice from horse back, the first round narrowly missed Elliott's hip. A second round hissed past his left ear with the energized heat almost searing it. He returned fire, cocking and firing the single action revolver twice, knocking the Indian off his horse.

Exhausted, Elliott dropped to his knees. *Reload, dammit! There may be others ...* He could scarcely hold the heavy revolver with both hands. The seething hatred and anger returned as he holstered a loaded revolver and drew his skinning knife. Stomping his boot heel into the backs of their heads, he grabbed their hair, pulled back hard and cut the hairline from ear to ear in the front and then around the back. With a mighty jerk, he ripped the scalps loose and off. He cut off their ears and private parts relegating them to an after life without reprieve, along with him.

He strung the bloody scalps on a leather thong and stood over the dead, mutilated bodies, holding the scalps in his outstretched right hand. He clenched them tightly, raised them above his head and screamed with all the air in his aching lungs at his God in the heavens above.

"Damn them all to Hell!" Sobbing, with tears streaming down his blood stained sweating face, he placed the leather thong with the scalps around his neck. He dropped his bloodied hands to his sides, and swore an oath to kill every Apache from that day forward.

The voice came again. "Hey, hombre. Help me." The outlaw tossed his revolver away.

Elliott stepped out from behind cover and approached the injured man's left side. He checked him carefully for other weapons. Finding none, he laid the man flat on the ground. The outlaw had lost a tremendous amount of blood. A shot had shattered the bicep and bone of the left arm.

Elliott leaned close. "Who murdered old man Williams and his cowpuncher? Was it Indio Chacon?

The bandit struggled to speak. "*Si.* You weel never .... catch Indio, *cabrón.*" And he died.

CHAPTER THREE

Joaquin Campbell rode up to Cienega Creek with his friend Carmen Ponce. They had checked on the welfare of his father's cattle on the north end of their ranch, riding all day. Heat waves shimmered over the desert landscape. It was past mid-day. Joaquin swung down from his paint horse. Disheveled dark hair peeked out from under his Stetson; his boyish face had a ready smile as he peered down at the inviting swimming hole. They allowed their horses to drink and tied them to mesquite trees along the bank.

"Wel-l-l now, would you just look at that cold water, Carmie. Time for a swim, I reckon."

Carmen hesitated, but before she could say anything, he stripped down and jumped into the water. Joaquin surfaced, blowing water into the air. "Come on in! The water's fine." She still hesitated, standing on the creek bank. *That's odd; we always like to swim in our favorite swimming hole.* He dove under the cold water again, broke the surface of the water refreshed, and let out a wild yell. He looked for his friend; she was walking quickly into the water toward him, and she looked absolutely beautiful. She was naked and her brown body seemed alive in the hot sun. He looked longingly at her body, noting the differences. He continued to stare at her.

She suddenly submerged herself in the water and swam away from him.

"Carmie, I ... I'm sorry. I didn't mean to stare. You're something special. It won't happen again."

"Joaquin, can't you address me as Carmen? I'm not a little girl any more you know."

"Why ... sure. Carmen it is then."

She would not look up at him but rather looked down into the water. He wanted so badly to go to her, but he knew somehow that he shouldn't. It wasn't the time. She started to speak then paused, pursing her lips.

What is it, Carmen? What's wrong?

"It's just not the same as all the times before, Joaquin. We're older now, growing into ..." Her voice trailed off and she began again, "We can't be doing this sort of thing anymore. It's not right. Besides, I'm just a Mexican."

Joaquin looked her straight in the eye. "You're right Carmen. I just didn't think. I'm sorry if you're embarrassed, but you've got to know I would never harm you in any way ... *ever.* And as far as you being Mexican, you're family to me and always will be." He paused, biting at his lower lip. "No ... you're much more than that to me. You're my best good friend, and as to the other—White or Mexican doesn't make a person good or bad."

She looked directly into his eyes, and he noticed a sadness he had never seen there before.

"You are the finest, kindest person I have ever known in my eighteen years on this earth. I love you Joaquin, more than you'll ever know. Someday, I may be asked to give my life for you. If that day ever comes, I will do it for you without any doubt or hesitation. For now, we must never tell anyone about this day or it will mean trouble for you and my father. And this ... must *never* happen again." She looked up at him again, her big brown eyes glowing, piercing his very being. "We're not little kids playing games anymore. We have grown up, Joaquin."

He swam out to where she was standing in the water. He took her hand in his and together they walked out of the water and up on the bank to their clothes. They dressed without speaking and silently rode home. They never spoke of the incident to anyone. It was their little secret, just as Carmen had said it would be.

Joaquin Campbell stuck his head further into the milk cow's flank and shouted, "Doggone it Molly, I said quit it! Stop tryin' to kick me now. I done spilled most of the milk outta this here bucket with your carrying on—*stop it!*"

The cow seemed to relax somewhat and at least quit struggling with the rope that Joaquin had tied around her legs near the hocks to keep her from "cow-kicking" him while he sat on the milk stool attempting to milk her. Quickly taking advantage of a lull in the action, he finished by stripping each teat between his thumb and forefinger. He reckoned he had almost a full bucket to take to the house for morning breakfast. Shoot, he even had enough to feed the new "doggie" calf in the barn.

He took the rope off Molly's hocks, released the stanchion lock, and fed her some hay. Then he poured half of the milk into a smaller bucket and walked over to a little calf penned in the corner of the barn.

"Well now little feller, lookee here at what I got for you."

Joaquin had found the cow calving yesterday by chance. He pulled the calf with great difficulty and was able to save it but not the mother. She had worn herself out over many hours of trying to give birth. He looked fondly down at the calf, a smile toying at his mouth. The calf tried to stand up, fell down, and stood again, wobbling back and forth. Joaquin stood over him and inserted his finger in the calf's mouth. The little guy immediately began sucking on his finger. He then lowered his finger in the milk bucket. When the milk was completely gone, the calf didn't seem to wobble. Joaquin rubbed him down with hay making sure he stayed dry and warm inside the barn. He picked up the other bucket of milk and headed for the ranch house.

As Joaquin stepped out of the barn, he shivered. A northerly wind whipped at his old wool jacket and pulled at his felt hat. Winter would be here soon. He was eighteen years old and just happy to be living with his parents on one of the best ranches along Cienega Creek in the Arizona Territory. The sun rose in the east over the top of the rugged Whetstone Mountains with an orange magnificence found only in the Arizona desert country. Joaquin could see the outline of the Rincon Mountains to the north with the protruding pinnacle, Rincon Peak, jutting out in the pale sky. To the west the Santa Rita Mountains, another small mountain range, appeared close but he knew they were, in fact, many miles away.

As he turned to head toward the house, Biscuit Mountain beckoned to him from the south along with the remaining Mustang Mountains. He surely loved this place. To him at that moment in December 1903, there was no place on earth known to him that could equal this ranch or his life with his family and friends.

Joaquin walked from the barn to the chicken coop, carrying his bucket of milk carefully in the wind. He stopped and watched a young Mexican girl feeding the chickens. He smiled at his best friend, Carmen Ponce. "Hey Carmen, how many *juevos* did you find today?"

She looked up quickly, her face flushed. "More than you can carry, *tonto*."

He threw back his head and laughed heartily. "*Yo creo que si. Tienes razon, mi amiga.* I reckon you're always right about things Carmen."

It was her turn to laugh. "I have twelve eggs for break-fast. Your mother will be happy today."

Joaquin had grown up with Carmen. She had always been there for him; playing with him when they were little children, and later, working with him and the others on the ranch.

The sunlight shone on Carmen's hair, two black braids that hung down the back of her wool jacket. She wasn't as tall as Joaquin, but he thought she was tall—for a girl—and skinny. ¡*Qué linda*! Just about right. She was something special all right. No doubt about it.

"*Oye*. We better get these eggs and that milk in to Marian or we'll be in big trouble." Startled from his thoughts, Joaquin realized that Carmen was speaking to him.

"*Bueno. ¡Vamos a desayunar!*" Joaquin responded hurriedly.

They laughed together and raced toward the warm ranch house, careful not to spill the milk or break any of the eggs.

CHAPTER FOUR

Joaquin opened the aging wooden door to the ranch house and stepped inside. He held it open with his boot allowing Carmen to slip past him into the warmth. Laughter still reverberated throughout the room. Two men sat at the kitchen table and were laughing heartily.

"Golly, Dad. You'd think that two grown men would be out working this time of the day."

Lou Campbell was a heavy-set man of average height for the day, with a face that had been chiseled out of living all his life in the outdoors and dealing with life threatening situations on a continual basis. He appeared even older than his sixty years implied with his white hair. He sat at the table with his friend and hired hand, Domingo Ponce.

Ponce was short, stocky, dark complected, with iron-gray hair gone white around the temples.

Joaquin's father leaned back in his chair. "I was just telling Domingo we'd be lucky to get enough milk and eggs in time fer breakfast with you two *chiquitos* lollygaggin' around all mornin'."

"*Es la verdad*," Domingo chimed in, chuckling again.

A middle-aged woman with her long brown hair pulled up into a bun was cooking flannel cakes on an old wood cook stove. She gestured at Joaquin. "Get the strainer cloth out, son, and get thet milk strained into the pail yonder. Your dad wants to get started working them calves today." Then she smiled at Carmen. "Carmen honey, you bring them eggs o'er here and cook 'em in this here fryin' pan fer these hungry men."

"*Si, Señora*." Carmen walked to the stove and cracked eggs into the heated frying pan. "Will Megan be here tonight after school, Marian?"

"She'll be here sure enough, *mïja* ...with her little Timmy. You lookin' to do more schoolin' with her?"

"Yes ma'am. She's been so kind to help me with school and learning English. I know she's tired after teaching those kids at the school house all day, tending to Timmy and all."

Marian looked at Carmen. "No child, she loves you, being around you, helping you. She wouldn't have it any other way." She flipped flannel cakes over in the skillet. "Folks around here are wrong not to let the Mexican kids go to school with the White kids. 'Course you're getting' first hand teachin' here at the house, I reckon."

"Yes ma'am, I know, and I truly owe Meg for that."

Lou spoke up. "You owe no one, girl. It's us thet owes you fer all your hard work and friendship ... along with your pa."

Marian and Carmen served everyone breakfast with fried eggs and flannel cakes. Lou swallowed down some hot coffee and licked his lips. "We need to get them calves branded today—the ones we missed in the fall roundup." He took another drink of his coffee. "Carmen, get them hogs fed and the wood over to the corral fer brandin'. Will ya git a good fire started? Branding irons are in the tack room." He peered over his cup at his son. "Joaquin, you get our saddle horses ready. Me and Domingo got some things to talk over; we'll be out shortly."

"Yessir. I'll get to it right away."

Lou stood with Domingo and looked around the room, directing his comments to everyone. "Everyone goes out-side ranch headquarters armed with a rifle from here on. There's bad people about; bandits, outlaws with a price on their heads. A couple months ago, Chacon's bunch ambushed ol' man Williams, killed 'im and his puncher then stole his stock. The Rangers tracked 'em down, killed the outlaws, 'cept Chacon. They got most o' them cows back, but they lost a good Ranger, Carlos Ayala. Thet damn Chacon gunned him down in cold blood. So be on the lookout and if trouble starts, run for home. No cow is worth gettin' yourself killed fer, yah hear?"

Carmen gasped, her sad brown eyes wide with fright.

Joaquin placed his arm around her shoulders. "It'll be alright, Carmie." *Oh no, I forgot to call her Carmen.* But she didn't seem to mind.

CHAPTER FIVE

J oaquin eased out into the middle of the corral with the horses milling around and trotting away from him. He opened the lariat loop in his right hand and held it ready against his left side. Picking out his father's big bay gelding with the white stockings, he walked forward and laid the hoolahand throw quickly and softly over his head. It floated out in the air in front of the bay circling the corral away from Joaquin. The big loop nestled around the horse's neck.

"Got ya, you ol' rascal!"

Joaquin reeled the horse in close, slipped the bridle with the snaffle bit deftly into the horse's mouth and the worn headstall over his ears. He then buckled the throatlatch, removed his lariat, led the horse outside the corral and tied him to the hitch rail. As he headed back to the corral for Domingo's horse, his dog barked loudly and looked out beyond the ranch headquarters to the south.

"Well now, Solo Vino. Have we got us a rider coming in?"

The old dog had just appeared one day around six years ago, and stayed on, winning the affection of the entire family. He turned out to be an excellent "watch dog" and an even better stock dog for working cattle. Joaquin narrowed his eyes to better view the approaching lone horseman. Solo Vino; he came alone. Yep, that dog was worth his weight in gold as a worker all right, but even more so as his faithful companion for all these years. The old dog was always there for him no matter what. Kinda like family, he thought.

Coiling his lariat then shaking out a sizable loop for catching the next horse, he could now see the approaching horse and rider clearly. They appeared almost as one and he knew only a few men other than his father who could fit that bill. The man rode easily, straight and tall in the saddle, his heels down with his weight slightly forward. Joaquin recognized the horse, a *grulla* or off colored bay. Viento— what a magnificent horse. Joaquin dropped his rope and ran toward the rider, forgetting his work.

"Dad ... Mom! Elliott's here!"

The rider slowed his mount to a walk as he approached the out buildings. The horse pranced sideways and appeared to eye the dog with a contemptuous look. Elliott brought him back gently into compliance. Then the animals recognized each other. The now-quiet old dog wagged his tail and inched closer to the horse and rider. Elliott reined his horse in close to Joaquin, swung his right leg over the saddle horn and pommel, to lean forward.

"*¿Como esta, mi'jo?*" The voice was gentle and full of warmth.

"I'm fine, Elliott. Gosh, it's so good to see you again. It's been awhile since you was last here." Joaquin shuffled his feet as he resisted the urge to push forward and hug this man—this good friend—as he had on many occasions as a young boy. He thought Elliott was not a large man just tall and lean, hardened by a lifetime of outdoor living. His thick, short hair was mostly gray and white as was his mustache. He wore a faded blue, long-sleeved shirt with a silver, five-pointed star displayed over the left pocket under a light wool jacket. His fringed shotgun chaps showed years of wear. He wore a pistol belt fully loaded with .45 cartridges; the holster nestled on his right side with a leather sheath and skinning knife on the left side. The aged holster and belt were oiled down with skunk grease. Encased in the holster was a well-used single action Colt .45 revolver; the brown butt displaying a worn inscription, "*M y J*". The revolver and holster hung high on his waist.

I reckon it has at thet, *mijo.*" Elliott looked thoughtfully at Joaquin with his piercing blue eyes.

"You've growed up to be a helluva fine lookin' young man. I'm shore proud o' ya ... real proud." He removed his leg from the saddle horn and swung easily off his horse, dropping the reins to the ground. Viento stood still as though the reins had been anchored to the ground where his master dropped them.

Elliott tipped his old battered Stetson back on his head, walked forward and embraced the young man, slapping him gently on the back. "Where's your folks, Domingo and Carmen, *mijo?*

Joaquin felt the hard Colt revolver beneath Elliott's wool jacket where it was secured in a leather shoulder holster on his left side. He shivered, thinking of the imposing deadliness of this man that he and his family had called a close friend for so many years.

"In the house 'cept for Carmie ... uh ... Carmen. She's ..."

"Elliott! *¡Que gusta me da en verte* !" Carmen ran at him from behind the barn and hugged him.

"Wel-l-l ... now. Let me take a looksee." Elliott held her out at arm's length, surveying the young girl. "Why, you're shore a purty one ... the purtiest gal west of the Mississippi River!"

Lou Campbell's deep voice of Lou Campbell reverberated from the porch.

"Howdy Elliott! You're a sight fer sad eyes. You doin' ranger work today or do ya have some time off fer doin' some real work?"

"I reckon I got me a few days off to do whatever pleases me, *compañero*. I ain't so shore 'bout work though." Elliott's deeply tanned face broke into a grin and his eyes twinkled.

"I tell you what, Lou. If Marian still makes some of them ex-tree special flannel cakes and eggs, why ... I'll trade ya room, board and mah good company fer any work ya want done."

Grinning, Lou nodded his approval and turned to his wife standing behind him in the doorway. "Marian, you reckon you can rustle up some food fer this ole friend o' ours?"

She stepped forward with her hands on her hips and smiled at the visitor.

"Get thet skinny body in here right now; we'll get you fattened up for all the hard work that Lou has planned for you today."

"Thank ya, Marian. I'll do just thet."

She turned to go into the house, then spoke over her shoulder. "Oh, you ... uh ... won't be needin' them guns of yours in *my* house."

Elliott hesitated, the silence hung uncomfortably in the air. His soft voice returned, "Yes ma'am. Reckon I'll put my gear in the barn and sleep there like always."

Domingo Ponce stepped out on the porch, embraced Elliott and said in Spanish, "Welcome, my friend. It's always good to see you."

"*El gusto es mío, amigo,*" replied Elliott.

Lou turned to follow his wife into the ranch house, "Elliott, git your gear stowed and somethin' to eat. We'll meet you out in the corral when you're done."

The old Ranger had already picked up the reins to his horse and was leading him toward the barn.

CHAPTER SIX

Joaquin's father and Elliott worked methodically back and forth, taking their time and then snaking their lariats out, heeling the calves and dragging them back one at a time. He and Domingo flanked them and held them for branding, castration, and ear marking.

His sister Megan arrived and assisted in the latter duties. Her son Timmy kept the branding fire going with Carmen running the hot irons back and forth and trading off with Megan occasionally. Joaquin watched Timmy. The boy stoked the fire from a large pile of wood adjacent to where he sat on the ground. His homemade wooden crutches lay next to him. Joaquin recalled his nephew contracting polio. The boy was sick for a long time and almost died, then was crippled for life. Megan and Timmy lived in the quarters provided at the back of the school house. She taught the local ranch kids how to read, write, and do arithmetic.

Timmy looked up, and seeing his uncle gazing at him, smiled broadly at him as he tossed more wood on the fire. Joaquin thought, *pobrecito; no ... no, Timmy never thinks of himself that way; shame on me for thinkin' it.*

Elliott eased his horse over next to Timmy, coiled his lariat and stepped down. "Get your beady butt up on ol' Viento an' take him fer a ride, boy."

"No—no thanks, Elliott. I better tend to the fire. It's the job my Mom assigned me to do today."

"Wel-l-l now ... I reckon I kin understand them orders bein' in the Army an' all, but ya see ... your mom ain't the head honcho out here." He slapped the coiled rope against his chaps. "No siree ... *I* am. And I ain't takin' no fer an answer." He dropped the rope and lifted the boy up and into the saddle. Immediately, the gray horse with the black mane and tail knew to obey his new rider. Timmy laughed as he hung on to the saddle horn. The boy was so happy and excited. Joaquin thought it was a doggoned good day to work and play with those he truly loved and admired.

The night air was cool but not cold. It was just right for sitting out on the porch with a jacket or a blanket. Joaquin pulled the collar of his wool jacket up and closer to his ears. All of them sat outside on the porch together enjoying the evening after supper. Lou, Domingo, and Elliott sat nearby, arguing Arizona politics, while the women discussed Megan's work at the school.

Elliott stood up and swatted at Timmy's hair. "I swear ... you look jest like your daddy—Gawd rest his soul. He shore was a mighty fine lookin' gent."

"I wish he was still alive and here with me."

"I know, son. But the fact is he ain't." Elliott reached again and patted the boy on the head.

Megan spoke up, "Elliott, do you think we might talk in private?"

Puzzled, he said. "Shore thing, Meg." They walked away from the porch toward the corral and barn. Joaquin's mother took Timmy inside; Domingo and Carmen retired to their house for the evening.

Joaquin looked over at his father, who was drinking from a tin cup filled with hot coffee and sitting in an old wooden rocking chair that he had made several years ago. "Does Elliott have another name? I mean I've never heard anybody over the years call him anything but—Elliott."

"Does thet bother you, son?"

Joaquin chewed on that thought for a while. "No, I reckon not. I just wondered is all."

"Well, I reckon he does have a first name same as all o' us. Most likely recorded somewheres back in Texas. Thet's where he come from, where I first met him when we was both younger men. He was about your age from what I recollect, maybe a tad younger."

Lou set his coffee cup down near his chair, reached in his shirt pocket for his "makins", and withdrew his can of Prince Albert tobacco and rolling papers. He prepared the paper and added just the right amount of tobacco, licked the paper and sealed it. Placing the newly made cigarette in his mouth, he reached down and retrieved a match from his pocket, brought it up sharply along his pants leg and completed lighting his cigarette. He drew on the cigarette and slowly exhaled the smoke. His dark face was pensive, delving deep into the past, remembering people and events of long ago.

"Ya see, son ... after the War Between the States there was a big market for cattle raised in Texas. In them days, prices fer cows was way more'n what a man could git in Texas. People figured out right quick thet them cows could be driven to Kansas and farther to Colorado and Wyoming. Why, they was shipped all the way to Chicago on the railroad and then later west to California, an' fer a nice profit. I was some older than Elliott. I made Trail Boss over time and hired Elliott at a saloon in San Antonio. We drove them herds jest 'bout ever' where in them days. He warn't no more'n fifteen years old then, but he was a man doin' a man's job. Why, he worked all day an' night. I never once heerd him complain or not do his part an' more."

Joaquin leaned toward his father as he sat on the porch. "Does Elliott have a family? Was he ever married?"

Lou drew again on his cigarette, the end glowed a bright red, illuminating a face completely lost in another place and time. "It was in Santa Fe thet Elliott met this here Spanish gal. The purtiest gal I ever seen anywhere—dark hair 'an eyes ... a daughter to some well-to-do feller. He owned a big ranch up in northern New Mexico Territory. Well, the short of it is they fell in love. I cain't recollect when thet was, but I'd say it was around '70.

Lou's face glowed like his cigarette only moments before. He dropped it by his feet and stepped on it without realizing what he had done.

"Life on the trail was tough and you either was man enough to live through it ... or you was daid. Toward the end o' trailin' herds, we moved a bunch o' them Texas long-horns from El Paso over to California. And we went plumb through this here Arizona Territory. Me an Elliott, we liked the lay of the land, and we seen right off thet it was good country for raising cows 'cept for one thing—Injuns. We had hell with 'em right off. Them Chiricahua Apaches was a handful. Ol' Cochise was running things in them days, and he had a passle o' warriors to play hell with anyone fool enough to try an' settle in Arizona. You was fair game fer 'em if you was caught out by yourself. We thought about a big cattle ranch, but with the Injun sit-i-a-tion and all ... why, it woulda been foolhardy. Hell, they stole our cows when we was runnin' them through goin' west with a bunch of tough men to take care o' the herd."

"What happened with the Spanish girl, Dad? Did they marry?"

Lou rocked back and forth in the old wooden chair; he frowned, pursed his lips, "I'm gittin' to thet, son." He paused, gathering his thoughts that had been briefly interrupted.

"As I was sayin'... Elliott ... an' thet purty gal ... they jest couldn't stand not being together all the time. I'm thinkin' her name was Maria. If'n you ever take a gander at them pistols thet Elliott wears, you'll see thet she and the boy's initials are on 'em.

"What boy? They *did* get married then, huh, Dad," Joaquin queried.

"Jest hold your hosses. They figgered to get hitched, but her ol' man was daid set 'agin it, bein's he thought she could do better an' all. Maria shore never seen it thet away. She seen right off thet Elliott was a real good man, shore 'nough special. They run off together, got married by thet padre over at San Xavier Mission. Elliott found a small spread along the San Pedro River and run a few head of cows. I stopped off to see 'em once on my way back from runnin' a herd over to California." A smile settled over Lou's craggy face. "They was real happy, an' had 'em a new son; they named him Joaquin. Thet's where me an' your mom come up with your name, son." The smile faded into a frown, wrinkling his leathery face. "Not long after thet a raidin' party o' Injuns come by the ranch when Elliott away from the house."

"What happened? Where are his wife and son?"

"I ain't goin' to talk 'bout it. You ask Elliott, son. Maybe he'll tell ya ... maybe he won't. But it's his job to do thet, I'd say."

"But ...Dad ..."

Lou's eyes squinted, his jaws clenched together; he took a deep breath, and let it out slowly. "Elliott went plumb nuts when he come home. He tracked them Injuns down, killed 'em all. After thet, he just warn't the same man. There was a burnin' kind o' hate thet jest kept eatin' away inside 'im. And he wouldn't never let go of it."

He looked over at his son. "Shore you're up for the rest of the story? It's a mite long at thet."

"My God; Dad, I've got to hear it all now!"

Lou finished his coffee and built another cigarette taking his time. He drew deeply on the cigarette and settled back in his rocking chair. "Well, Elliott left the ranch pretty much like it was. I reckon its still there fer 'im to come back to someday. He went off and joined the U.S. Army. They was jest startin' to do somethin' in them days 'bout hostile Injuns in the Arizona Territory. He signed on an' worked with the scouts under one of the Chiefs of Scouts, Merejildo Grijalva. All he could think of was killin' Injuns, an' I reckon he done jest thet.

"Later, after he left the Army, he hired out his gun. Lord only knows how he survived all thet bloodlettin'. He'd disappear fer awhile then show up at our ranch. When the war with Cuba broke out, he come by one day and asked if I'd go fight them Spaniards with 'im. You remember boy; thet's not been more'n five years ago. Your mom ... she warn't happy atall with Elliott on thet one, but I went with him an' the Arizona Rough Riders. We was in Troop A with Bucky O'Neill as our captain."

Joaquin listened intently, caught up in the story. He suddenly realized he had not moved. Being uncomfortable, he moved his buttocks ever so slightly, not wanting to break his father's concentration. "Elliott ... would never hurt any of us, would he?"

"No son. He's a hard man; tough as nails, but at the same time he's one of the finest men thet I've ever knowed."

"But, he killed all those people. It don't even sound like the Elliott I know."

"I don't know if I kin explain it, son. He had changed some by the time we went to Cuba. It was like he had figgered out thet he had done wrong, made amends to Gawd fer it ... and well, was a better man fer it."

"So why did you, Elliott and all the others go to Cuba then? I mean with Mom so sore and all?"

"We all believed then, and I still do, thet we had to stand up fer the *United* States o' America after them Spanish bastards blew up the *Maine*. With ol' Teddy Roosevelt runnin' things, we done all right, I reckon." Lou rubbed the stubble on his chin, closed his eyes. "As fer Elliott, he was a helluva Rough Rider. There was—a calmness about him— he didn't care if he lived or died.

"Why not, Dad?"

"You'll hafta ask *him* 'bout thet." Lou cleared his throat. "Them Spaniards left snipers in the trees and thick brush. They had .45 caliber rifles with smokeless powder. They'd fire on jest about any target, but mostly our medics and wounded soldiers headed fer the rear. Sometimes, they shot at our couriers and water details. Anyhow, ol' Teddy Roosevelt, he didn't cotton much to thet atall. He handpicked thirty sharpshooters from our regiment to track them bastards down and kill 'em. Elliott and me, we was a team. It was dirty work and dangerous. We hunted 'em in pairs. We'd find us a sniper an' one o' us would circle around ... *real* careful like, lettin' the sniper see you from time to time; the idea bein' *not* to get shot. Them snipers would move or take a shot, an' your pard, who was hidin' in a good spot not too fer off, would shoot the son-of-a-bitch dead."

"Did you take turns movin' and shootin'?" asked Joaquin.

"I wanted to at the time son, but Elliott, he wouldn't have none o' thet. He jest grinned, said he had been fightin' Injuns fer so many years an' was the best Injun crawler. He said I couldn't move as fast as him ... thet I had a family to look after." Lou paused, rubbing his forehead. "We killed eleven Spanish guerrilla snipers thet first day with none o' us bein' hurt atall." He stood up, stretched his frame and yawned, signaling that the storytelling was coming to an end.

Joaquin jumped up next to his father. "Dad, come on,

tell me more ... please!"

"Well, maybe *mañana,* boy. I'm plumb tuckered out. I think I'll turn in." He started into the house, turned back, and looked straight into his son's eyes, "If you remember nothin' else I teach you son, remember this: All of us on this here earth have our time in the sun. We kin make something of it—or not. Every single day, each of us kin choose to make it a good day or a bad 'un. We kin choose to do right, treat others with respect, an' live a good, clean life. Believe me boy, life goes by mighty fast." Lou reached out and hugged Joaquin close, patting him affectionately on his back. *I love you so much, Dad—always have, always will.*

"And Elliott; has he done that, Dad?" Joaquin asked.

"Thet an' more, son. He may have got a little sidetracked early on, but he's gittin' back on the right track. Saved my life in Cuba. Elliott was always puttin' other lives first. He and them Rangers are cleanin' this territory of rustlers and outlaws so it'll be a better place to live and raise a family." He sighed deeply and turned to go inside.

"Good night, son. I love ya. Reckon I'll see ya in the mornin'."

"Yessir ... in the mornin' then."

Lou reached for the screen door as he heard his son say, "I love you, too." He didn't respond, but a smile appeared, wrinkling his weathered face as he opened the door and entered the house.

CHAPTER SEVEN

egan Campbell gently took Elliott's arm and led him off in the direction of the corral. She had wanted to speak with him alone for sometime, and she did not want this golden opportunity to slip from her grasp. The clear night sky was full of stars twinkling down on them; a cool, crisp breeze blew through her hair as a full moon illuminated their surroundings making it relatively easy to walk without a lamp.

Elliott was mostly silent as usual around her, listening to her talk. She stopped him near the corral, well away from the house. She paused in conversing, allowing him an opening, "You look tired tonight, Meg. You ain't workin' too hard are ya?"

"I feel so much older these days, Elliott. I don't know how *not* to work hard." She laughed aloud, a short strained laugh. "You know how I was raised at home. It's just so very important to me that *all* of the children be educated. It's so unfair that only the white children are allowed in the school."

"But ..." Elliott knew the answer before she responded.

"I just can't *stand* the extreme prejudices of some of the school board members and the general community as well. They simply will not allow the Mexican children into the school with the whites. Shame on them."

Elliott edged closer. "Meg, I'm shore glad you're doin' sech a fine job with them youngsters. I heerd you got the board to allow you to teach them Mexican kids on Saturdays.

Ya done good. The future of this territory is in them kids and their schoolin'. Why, the better for all of us, I reckon."

Shuddering at his grammar, she bit her tongue at correcting him for she knew in his day a man went to work when he came of age and that education had not been important. With the exception of her father, she respected Elliott more than any man. She liked—no, she loved him—for what he was, not how he spoke or the clothes he wore. He was a good kind man, who came from a sad, violent past. He had always been there for her and Timmy when others looked away and did nothing. *God bless him for that.*

"Elliott, I must talk to you about something ... well ... something you might feel I shouldn't discuss with you." The breeze had picked up some and she wished she had tied her hair back. She hesitated, brushing her dark brown hair out of her eyes. He looked directly at her with those piercing blue eyes.

"Wel-l-l now, Meg, I'd say jest spit it out. I ain't never not listened to you, have I?"

She smiled up at him, trying not to think of the double negatives he had just spoken, and returned his gaze. "It's about my brother."

He frowned; his tongue appeared between his lips and toyed with his white mustache, one side then the other. "Why? There somethin' I should know?"

"Well ... uh ... he's doing fine. It's not that, I mean ..."

He tensed slightly, "Don't play games with me, Meg. I'm too damned old."

"Joaquin is almost nineteen years old. He's become a man, Elliott."

"Yessir ... I reckon so," he drawled.

" What I mean is ... he needs someone to talk to him ... *you know* ... about women and ... uh ... well, you know, the birds and the bees, so to speak."

He took a sudden step backward, almost tripping, started to turn then changed his mind and stuttered, "What the hell ... *what are ya askin', Meg?*"

Megan kept her voice soothing. "You're the perfect person to talk to him. Elliott, Joaquin admires you. He truly cares about you and would listen to anything you had to say."

"Meg, you listen here now. First of all, I ain't the one who should be talkin' to Joaquin 'bout ... 'bout ... *skeedoodlin'* an' sech."

"Skeedoodling?" She frowned, her mouth dropped open.

"Well shore, you know a man and a woman doin' ... what ... uh ... they do together. *You know.*"

She almost laughed out loud when she realized he was serious. *Where on earth had he come up with that word?* She maintained her composure, "Well, *yes.* Exactly. Don't you see? You're already thinking about how to discuss the matter with him."

"The heck I am." roared Elliott. "Listen here, Meg. I ain't the right one. I mean his daddy ought to be the one. I got no right, no business ..."

"Don't you see, Elliott? You have *every* right. You're the one who *should* explain to him ... about ... skeedoodling; just like you said."

He stared at the ground, his face reddening, and shuffled his feet. "Meg, I ain't nobody to ... I mean, I made mistakes back many years ago ..."

"All the more reason you should be the one discussing this matter with him, my friend. He's definitely interested in girls now. One in particular, although he hasn't quite figured it out yet. He's been looking at Carmen differently than he used to, and she loves him. *I know it.*"

"Little Carmen? Naw. You're readin' way too much into thet gal."

"Well, anyway he needs some educating ... and soon. Dad won't talk to him about it. I know that much."

"I kin damn well understand thet," retorted Elliott.

She walked close to him and took hold of both arms. "He could get into trouble if someone doesn't help him. You know ...sexual disease ... someone pregnant or ..."

"Fer cryin' out loud, Meg." Elliott turned away, slapping his leg, paused and faced her. "Hell. All right, I'll talk to the boy."

She reached up and kissed him on the cheek, "Thank you, my friend."

He looked down at the ground and shuffled his boots again. "I'll get to it first thing in the mornin', if'n thet suits you, 'lil missy."

"Wel-l-l ..." She turned toward the ranch house porch where Joaquin sat on the porch alone. "Now's the perfect time, Elliott. Talk to him tonight. *Please*."

"Doggoned if you ain't persistent as all get out. Now's as good a time as any, I reckon. You go on to bed, Meg. I'll take care o' this here sit-i-a-tion tonight."

"Thank you, Elliott."

"You go on now, and send thet young lad on o'er here."

"Okay. There is one more *tiny* favor?"

He gazed intently at her with those piercing blue eyes once again. They softened and twinkled as he spoke, "Your bank account 'pears to be 'bout closed out, I'd say. What is it Meg?"

"Well, Joaquin is taking Carmen to the dance in Sonoita tomorrow night, and I was wondering if ... maybe you would ... well, that is ... if you would take me with you?" Then she said quickly, "We could all go together."

He hesitated. "You probably wouldn't want to be seen with an old widower like me." *Oh darn, I shouldn't have done that.* She turned slowly away from him with her head down.

"Whoa now! Jest hold your hosses, Meg. I'd be proud to take ya to the dance, but I ain't been dancin' fer a passle of years, an' to be honest with you, I warn't much good at it even back then."

"Oh, that doesn't matter. It will be fun going together, Elliott."

"We'll go I reckon, but don't you be tryin' to lead ... ya hear?"

It was difficult for her not to laugh out loud knowing that in the end she would indeed lead, and he would never be the wiser. She smiled up at him, "I wouldn't dream of trying it, my friend."

He watched as she walked back toward the house, to her brother sitting on the porch. He couldn't help thinking what a fine looking woman she was in her cotton dress. *Yep, she's a keeper fer shore.* All the years he had known her, she was so easy to be around; didn't make him fidgety 'atall. If a man didn't feel like talkin' ... why, that was jest fine with her. As he watched Joaquin strolling over to him, he imagined her in his arms on the dance floor. *Dadjimmit! What the heck am I thinking of her again fer anyhow?*

"Evening, Elliott." Joaquin walked up to him and leaned back against the corral railing. "Cooling down some, I reckon. Megan said you wanted to talk to me about something."

"*Buenos tardas, mi'jo.* I reckon I did want to palaver with you some. What do you say 'bout settin' a spell?"

"Sure, this okay right here?" Joaquin pointed at the ground next to the corral.

"It'll do ... I reckon." Elliott lowered himself to the ground with his back against the corral poles. Joaquin sat with his legs folded under him. They enjoyed several moments of a quiet evening; not talking, just listening to all the night sounds. The full moon lit up the desert landscape with a ghostly appearance, and all the bright stars seemed to be dancing in the sky. Elliott took out his "makin's," carefully built himself a cigarette, lit it, and exhaled slowly. "Joaquin, you and me ... we've knowed each other fer a lot of years. *¿Qué no?*"

"For longer than I can remember."

"You reckon you kin trust in what I tell ya?"

"Yessir."

Elliott hesitated then continued, "I never had the chance to talk to mah own son 'bout bein' a man, *skee*doodlin' an' sech."

"Why is that, Elliott?"

"He was kilt by Injuns when he warn't but a little feller." He cleared his throat, swallowed hard. "The sumbitches bashed his head 'agin a rock."

"I'm so sorry."

"No need to be, *mijo*. He and his mother... they're in a much better place now. I've learned thet much over the years, I reckon." Elliott nodded his head as if in agreement with himself.

Joaquin shuffled his position on the ground, cleared his throat, "Elliott ... I ... uh ... skeedoodling? I'm not sure what you mean."

"*Skeedoodlin'* boy. What a man an' a woman do." He thought for a moment. "Well, thet is when they're married." He drew hard on his cigarette then he put it out in the cool soil beneath his boot heel.

"Thet's why you an' me are havin' this here 'lil talk. I reckon Meg's plumb worried with you bein' a man ... bein' interested in them gals an' all."

Elliott leaned in close to Joaquin, gesturing with his hands. "I reckon you most likely seen thet women is built diffrent than men?" He continued without waiting for an answer. "You recall thet trip to Phoenix with me and your dad 'bout a year ago?"

"Yessir. We stayed at that big hotel—the Adams Hotel."

"Shore 'nough, boy. You recall it had thet fancy plum-min' we was all gawking at?"

"Yes sir. They had running water and toilets. Pretty fancy ... beat the heck out o' our privy and water bucket here at the ranch."

"Good boy. Do you recall us lookin' at them pipes an' seein' how some fit into others?"

Joaquin frowned. "Yessir. I remember."

Elliott smiled and breathed a sigh of relief. "Wel-l-l now ... thet's the short of it, boy. I reckon you got the jest of it alright."

Joaquin had a puzzled look on his face. "I'm sorry Elliott. I'm not sure I understand."

Elliott sighed, his shoulders slumping. *How kin I explain this? Gawd, give me the doggoned words.* "Why ... don't you *see* boy? The plummin's different fer men and women, just like them pipes. The man pipes fit into the woman pipes." He looked directly at Joaquin for his confirmation. "Do I hafta spell it out fer ya, boy?"

Joaquin's mouth dropped open. Then he nodded. "No sir. I think I understand now."

"Good boy. Now, stay with me, there's more." Joaquin's eyes widened.

"When you git away from home, you're gonna be tempted to *skee*doodle with a woman. I'm here to tell ya to be mighty careful. Why, ya don't want to be doin' thet with no one 'cept the woman ya marry one day. You'll likely git some gal with child fer shore. Bad doins." He paused, his face pensive, "Another thing ... they got whore houses jest 'bout ever' where in the territory. Don't be gittin' tempted in them places neither. You'll catch the clap ... or worse."

"The clap?"

"A disease ya get from them whores. You hurt bad when ya pass water an' then there's the sif-e-us. Thet there is *muy malo*, Joaquin. I've seen men ... an' women walkin' around with sores—sick to death, son. You jest recall what I told ya an' steer clear of them places; you'll be alright, I reckon." Elliott gazed off into the distant horizon. *Hell bells, this here was goin' better'n he thought it would.*

"Sure, Elliott."

"Another thing you remember, *mi'jo*. You'll likely be drinkin' some o' thet rotgut whiskey. And if'n ya drink too much, you'll be tempted to git with them women 'cause ya ain't got your head screwed on straight. An' there's always some of the men ya ride with badgering ya on, but you be a bigger man, Joaquin—you do what's *right*." He looked into Joaquin's eyes.

"You care fer Carmen, *mi'jo?*"

"What?"

"You heerd me, boy."

"She's my best friend ... you know that. She has been there all my life that I can remember."

"I figgered as much, Joaquin. But do you *love* her?"

"Yessir ... as much as anyone can love another, I reckon."

"Meg thinks Carmen loves you, too." His right leg aching, Elliott rolled to his left knee and stood, and stretched his tall frame. Joaquin stood, dusting himself off.

"She doesn't think she's for me 'cause she's Mexican." Joaquin sighed, "I've told her it don't matter, Elliott. We are who we are, not because of the color of our skin, but who we are inside ... here." He pointed at the center of his chest.

Elliott thought about what the boy said and again of his own past; all the water under the bridge, those years so long ago. He took Joaquin by the shoulders and squared him around.

"You're shore right. Thing is there's plenty o' others in this here world that don't agree with you none atall. They kin make livin' pure hell fer ya if'n ya let 'em. I reckon I know something 'bout it, bein' married to a Mexican gal myself fer a spell. I've shore seen mighty good folks an' worthless sons-a-bitches on both sides o' the aisle. Truth is you an' Carmen will hafta figger out what you want all by your lonesome. If'n it's what both o' ya want, why ... thet's all thet matters. I'll stand with ya, *mijo*...with both o' ya, an' be proud to!"

Joaquin pulled the collar of his wool coat up around his ears. The night was cooling off quickly. He held out his hand to his good friend. *"Muchas gracias, mi amigo. Despues hablamos más."*

As they turned toward the house, Elliott placed his arm around the boy's shoulder. Walking together, the old ranger and the young man appeared as one, distinctly silhouetted by a bright moon under a clear southwestern sky. Times seemed uncertain for the two of them in that beautiful but dangerous territory called Arizona, but that night nothing seemed insurmountable.

CHAPTER EIGHT

J oaquin watched Carmen as she appeared on the porch
of the ranch house dressed in pants, wool jacket, gloves
and hat. He grinned at her. "Hey, better get a move on if
you're wantin' to ride with us, kid."

She looked at him, waiting beside her horse, then over
at Elliott and Megan already mounted and ready to ride.
She quickly dropped off the porch and ran to the horse,
stepping into the ready-made stirrup of Joaquin's interlaced
fingers and hands. As he gently lifted, she vaulted easily
into the saddle, taking the reins and control of the skittish
gelding. "*Gracias*, Joaquin."

"*De nada.*" His words drifted back over his shoulder as
he reached for the reins and swung up on the back of his
paint horse. The paint reared and pranced sideways.

Elliott's deep voice resounded in the cold air. "I reckon
we're all bundled up enough fer the trip." He reined Viento
up close to Megan. "I ain't so sure 'bout leavin' mah guns
Meg, but they'd be plumb in the way o' mah fancy dancin'
... thet's fer shore." He laughed heartily as the four of them
rode out toward town.

Although Elliott thought it was a mistake to leave his
pistols behind, he did think that Megan's son Timmy was in
mighty good hands staying behind with the grandparents.
He noticed that Megan had pulled her fine brown hair back
into a bun with a heavy scarf tight over her head and ears,

the free ends moving ever slightly in the breeze. *I'd like to see her hair loose ... flowin' down her back. Easy now ... ya ol' codger.* Lou an' Marian shore raised a fine daughter—and son. But Megan, she made him feel year's younger, and he liked being with her. How many days now till Christmas? Two days? No matter; it'd be here soon enough. He would buy Megan something special. But what? He decided to ask Carmen— she would know. Elliott watched in fascination as Carmen's dark, glossy hair, arranged into two braids, bounced against her back as she and Joaquin rode ahead of him.

They arrived in town after the long ride, their cheeks rose-colored from the cold night air, and left the horses at the livery stable. The four of them then walked down the street toward the town hall where the dance was being held. From outside in the street, Elliott heard fiddles playing coupled with raucous laughter and the sound of many feet on the dance floor. He took a deep breath of fresh air before following Joaquin and the two women into the dance hall.

The large room was packed full with men, women, and a few children who played in a crowded corner. The dancers were all dressed in their finest; their feet pounding the wooden floor in cadence with the fiddler's fast-paced music. As always, the wall-flowers sat dejectedly on benches along the walls, refusing to push aside their inhibitions to dance, thereby relegating themselves to an unhappy night. Elliott took all their coats and hats and moved carefully through the crowd to the coat room. He hung them together for an easy find later in the evening.

Walking back to where Joaquin stood with the two women, he saw a couple dancing in time with the music; the man embracing the woman with his right arm while holding her right hand in his left. They laughed together and disappeared in the melee on the dance floor. The men wore polished boots, their best cotton shirts and pants, some string bow ties and vests. The women who were fortunate enough to ride a buggy or wagon into town wore their finest cotton dresses reaching to the floor, atop their leather shoes. Those women arriving by horseback wore pants and boots.

A festive mood prevailed with participants dancing, conversing, and enjoying the festivities. The joy of Christmas was in the air and with it, a general feeling of fun and happiness. All the hard work and even harder times were forgotten, even for a short time, with the local folks trying their hand at dancing to the sound of fiddles and an occasional guitar.

Joaquin ventured out onto the dance floor with Carmen, trying to get the hang of it. Other couples banged and bumped into them; he was unsure of what he needed to do—just how to hold her, which direction to go. He thought it sure is crowded. Then he stepped on her toes. Startled at his own awkwardness, he jumped backward directly into another couple. "Sorry." He said over his shoulder then to Carmen, *"¡Lo siento mucho!"*

"It's okay, Joaquin. Quit worrying about the dancing and just follow me."

She showed him how to hold her with his right arm around her waist. He held her close, feeling the warmth of her, enjoying the scent of her hair. Looking into her big brown eyes, he smiled. Again, he bumped into someone on the dance floor, and looked up to see Elliott and Megan.

"Thet's the ticket, boy. You look like you was born to dance," Elliott drawled. Megan laughed aloud then the two of them disappeared into the dense sea of dancers. Joaquin mumbled another apology to Carmen. Somehow he would master this dancing thing here tonight, even if it killed him.

Although thoroughly embarrassed with his lack of

skill on the dance floor, he liked being with his best friend and learning how to complement the movements of her body. Carmen was so much fun to be with and she seemed to understand dancing so well. Megan had said earlier that Carmen was a good teacher, and by golly, she ought to know all about teaching. He held Carmen ever closer to him. It felt so natural, well worth the risk of dancing badly.

The music stopped for the musicians to take a breather. Joaquin thought it was like when their horses stopped to blow at the top of one of the steep hills while riding over to the dance.

"I need to wet my whistle, Carmen. Would you like some punch?"

"*Si, gracias Joaquin. Tengo mucha sed.*"

"I'll be right back. You just have a seat right here." He pointed at the wooden chair against the wall.

Carmen smiled at Joaquin, nodded her head, and turned to sit, watching Joaquin disappear into the crowd. Megan was such a life-saver, teaching her how to dance. Carmen still wasn't very good, but with Joaquin knowing almost nothing, she felt like she was the expert. *I'm having so much fun with him tonight. But then I always do. Always have.* She breathed in pure happiness. Her love for him had grown more and more each day. *What will become of us?* She had no idea, but for now, at this very moment, she just appreciated their time together.

Someone laughed loudly to her left then others snickered. Carmen had been so caught up in her own thoughts that she had failed to notice anyone nearby. She looked around quickly and saw four men standing against the wall, all of them staring directly at her.

One of the men pointed his index finger at her. His face was ruddy and he looked as if he were drunk. "Yeah ... *you,* Messican! How's 'bout me an' you dancin'?"

She looked around quickly for Joaquin, but did not see him. "I am sorry, *Señor.* I am here with someone else tonight."

The man stumbled over to where Carmen was sitting until he towered over her. Fear rose up in her throat. His pointed small eyes held a mean look, full of hatred, and his face contorted while his right eye twitched. The other men joined him laughing as he stood, teetering back and forth. Carmen could see his eyes were red and bloodshot. He leaned closer to her; his hot foul breath reeked of alcohol.

"Please *Señor* ... I do not wish for any trouble. As I said, I am here with someone."

The man straightened, looked around at all his friends, ensuring that he had their attention. "Wel-l-l, I don't see no one with ya. Just you an' me, cutie. Let's dance." He grabbed her arms and attempted to lift her from the chair.

She shook his hands off. "Keep your filthy hands off me! *Get away!*"

His expression hardened. With clenched teeth, he swayed forward unsteadily and slapped Carmen across the mouth. Spittle escaped from his mouth and ran down his unshaven chin.

"You greaser *bitch.* I don't ever take no from no Messican. Just who the *hell* do you think you are ... huh? Telling me no. By God, I'll take you out back where ya belong." He reached for Carmen again.

"That's enough!" The sharp-edged voice echoed and reverberated throughout the room.

Turning quickly toward the voice that had challenged him, the drunken man teetered unsteadily on his feet. Elliott met him almost face to face as he turned. Carmen saw the man squint his bloodshot eyes peering at the tall, white haired man facing him. Had he not been so drunk, he might have noticed the man facing him had bladed himself with his left foot forward and his right foot back; his feet apart about the width of his shoulders. Elliott had positioned himself in a good defensive position with the drunk between him and the other men. For the moment, Elliott did not have to worry about his back.

Carmen watched in horror, her face stinging. Elliott slapped the ruffian hard; the man stumbled backwards almost as fast as the resounding force of the blows were heard across the room. "Them *chingasos* feel good, *cabrón* ...*huh?*" Elliott's face grim, he stepped in closer to the stunned man.

"Who ... the hell are ya?" The man's reddened face transformed from bewilderment to outrage. Carmen could not find the words to speak. *Oh, my God. Elliott, watch out!* The ruffian swung hard with his right hand, a haymaker straight for the face of the older man confronting him. Elliott ducked under the punch, moved to his left, and brought his leg up almost to his chest, then straight down at a sharp angle. Elliott's boot struck the man's knee hard sideways. Her eyes wide, Carmen screamed. A strange popping sound and a curdling scream came from the man's lips. He fell to the floor, grasping his knee. Elliott again brought his leg up toward his chest as he turned sideways then kicked his leg out hard straight into the man's face. His boot heel caught the man directly in his face and slammed the drunk backwards onto the floor. Blood and several teeth flew from his mouth. His eyes rolled back in his head.

Elliott turned quickly to the others bunched to the side. "I'll *kill 'im* fer what he done." He stepped closer to the three men his face hard, determined. His voice rang out loud and clear in a room now full of silent people. "What's holdin' ya? Ya *sons-a-bitches*. Ya damn well didn't mind pickin' on thet 'lil girl o'er yonder."

One of the other two ruffians spoke up, "I remember you, mister ... from Bisbee, several years back." Elliott stood solid. The man's tongue appeared between his lips, toyed with his dried lips, the fear showing in his face. "Look mister, I don't want no trouble. "'Hit was Jed what harmed the girl."

"You was laughin', *cabrón!*"

The man swallowed hard. "I'm damned sorry fer it, too." He looked over at Carmen. "I'm sorry, ma'am. Real sorry."

One of the other men spoke up. "He's right, mister. We didn't mean nothin' ... *honest*. I'm sorry, too, ma'am."

The remaining ruffian spat at Elliott's feet. "Ya yella bellies. I ain't apologizin' to no Messican, you ol' bastard."

Elliott focused on the new threat. He waved his hand at the other two men, motioning them toward the door. "Go on ... *git*." After a moment's hesitation, the two men shuffled out the door. Carmen wrung her hands as tears ran down her face.

Elliott watched the man who had refused to apologize; he was standing over his unconscious companion on the floor. His right hand was behind him. Elliott knew the man would come out with either a gun or a knife. God willing, it would be a knife. His guns were back at the ranch.

The man sneered and brought his right hand forward. Elliott saw the large skinning knife. The man lunged at Elliott's belly with the blade.

Anticipating the move, Elliott kicked his right leg hard to the left, balancing on his left. His foot caught the knife arm squarely. The knife spun away. Elliott shifted his weight onto his right foot as he turned in a three hundred sixty-degree arch. Building his momentum, he swung his left leg. His heel cracked hard against the man's jaw.

The man was flung sideways then fell back to the floor and did not move. Elliott walked over and kicked the man, in the face then in the ribs. *I'll kill ya—ya* ... Carmen screamed again. Elliott heard movement behind him and turned quickly to confront a new threat. Joaquin came toward him with a puzzled, scared look on his face; he dropped the two cups of punch.

"Jeez, Elliott ... please don't hurt that man anymore. *¿Qué pasó?*" Frowning with his mouth open, he stared at the two prostrate men on the floor.

Elliott exhaled slowly, his eyes quickly viewing the entire room. His right knee throbbed. It was going to be a long ride back to the ranch with his bum knee re-injured. Elliott thought, *the boy's right, hoss ... ya can't kill 'im.* He took a deep breath and felt for the old wooden rosary tucked in his front pocket. *Ya promised—what would Maria think?*

"They was tryin' to be a might rough on Carmen, *mi'jo.*"

He looked for Megan and saw her sitting next to Carmen, comforting her. Carmen looked up at him, her eyes wide, and tears still streaming down her brown face. She swallowed hard and stammered, "Elliott, I'm so sorry. It was all my fault." She sobbed. Megan hugged her.

Elliott glared at the crowd of dancers standing around the room, his eyes blazing. "No, it warn't your fault, Carmen. These men got off easy tonight."

A metallic ring edged his voice. "Anybody else here got somethin' to say 'bout Carmen or any o' us, *spit it out.*" Elliott breathed hard, his fists clenched as his eyes bored into the faces of the crowd assembled in front of him.

Deathly silence prevailed in the room then a man spoke up, "She's more'n welcome in here, mister." Elliott's eyes blazed. After a moment, his rage spent, he sighed, the breath escaping slowly from his lungs. "Learn to accept folks fer what they are, *damn you!*"

Out of habit, he backed slowly toward the door, and the four of them slipped quietly out of the dance hall. The old Ranger limped toward the stables, and wondered just how in the hell he was still alive after all these years. *It's a damned wonder, hoss ... a damned miracle is what it was.*

CHAPTER NINE

Lou Campbell rode up the canyon looking for his cattle and any rustler sign. His rifle draped across the pommel of his saddle. After spotting plenty of strange horse tracks mingled with cow tracks a ways back, he'd sent Domingo Ponce to check the adjacent canyon. The bitter cold and wind with intermittent snow flurries accentuated an Arizona winter day in February. The overcast sky displayed a mixture of black and gray clouds adding dreariness to the already miserable day.

He pulled his Stetson down farther onto his head and pulled up the collar on his wool mackinaw jacket. The chaps and the tapadero stirrups provided him some respite from the cold that gnawed at him as he nudged his bay gelding up the canyon.

He couldn't help thinking how dangerous the times were. Not as bad as the old days some twenty or thirty years ago when the Apache had pretty much controlled the territory. But bad enough for him to worry about his family's safety. Indio Chacon's band came up regularly from Mexico—a force to be reckoned with for sure. If that wasn't bad enough, a lot of other hard cases in the territory hid out from the law and had no problem stealing a man's property or harming his family. These riffraff needed to be cleaned out so the territory could grow with honest, good people. Lou shook his head. Easier said than done. Would the Rangers be able to do that or would it fall to their kids?

It began to snow more heavily and he hunched forward slightly in his saddle to ward off the chill. *Joaquin.* The boy was a man now—a good man at that. He was so proud of him and what he had become, but he worried about the boy's relationship with Carmen. Just last night he'd told his son he should let his heart decide on whether to marry Carmen, but in the end, be prepared for some folks to dislike or even hate them for intermarrying. He told both of them that he, his mother, and Domingo would support them in any decision they made. Lou grimaced. *It ain't worth worrying 'bout them kinds of people.*

As he reached the head of the canyon, he observed the tracks of maybe thirty head of cattle mixed with two sets of shod horse tracks. They continued on over the next ridge to the south toward the adjacent canyon where Domingo was riding. He levered a cartridge into the rifle chamber and pushed the bay gelding up over the ridge at a trot with the rifle butt now riding on his right thigh. From his vantage point high on the ridge, he saw the tracks descending down the header canyon that eventually dropped into the larger arroyo, Apache Canyon. Lou squinted hard through the falling snow as he scanned the terrain, but he could not see anything moving in the distance.

He followed the tracks down the header canyon. Then he pulled back sharply on the reins and his horse stopped. He peered down at additional tracks, cattle and several more horses merging with the ones he had been following. Someone was pushing a hundred head or more of his beef down Apache Canyon. *Rustlers!* His heart beat quickened as he stared down at the sign on the ground. The tracks were not more than a half hour old. He was sure of that. *Domingo.* He would be riding directly into the rustlers from below. Lou did not hesitate, spurring his horse down into the deep canyon, sending snow and dirt flying. He had not gone far when he heard gunfire echoing up toward him as he descended.

Lou pushed his horse hard toward the sound of the shots. He peered through the low clouds and thickening snow—something for him to use in his favor. Leaning down low over his horse's neck, he raced into the canyon below, the horse's mane flicking his face. He looked hard at the landscape, straining his eyes looking for something ... anything ahead of him.

He heard more shooting then shouts. A horse and rider appeared in front of him, and turned too late, to confront him. Lou raised his rifle toward the shape of a large man wearing a black sombrero, when his horse slammed into the other horse and rider. He heard bone snap, the horse utter a high-pitched scream followed by an agonizing groan.

Lou sailed through the air over the head of his bay gelding. *The rifle ... hit ...roll viejo!* He hit the ground hard, jolted to the core. Rolling several times, he slammed into something hard—a large boulder. Lou flexed his legs and arms to check for injuries and focused on the rifle still in his hand. The wind had picked up. He squinted through the snow falling in thick, wet sheets from the dark sky. A few yard away, Domingo Ponce's sorrel stood, reins dropped to the ground. Domingo lay face down on the ground.

One of the rustlers stood over Ponce's body with a handgun. He turned toward Lou. Campbell raised his rifle and shot him twice. The man cried out, clutched his chest and fell backward to the snow-covered ground. Breathing hard, Lou stood up shakily. He hobbled as fast as he could toward his friend. Ponce was not moving. Blood trickled into the white snow, seeping fan-like from his friend's head. As Lou reached for Domingo, a bullet hit the ground near his boots as he knelt, spraying him with snow and dirt. A second round entered his left leg behind his knee, throwing him slightly forward. He wanted to scream from the stabbing, intense pain, but he somehow choked it back. Turning toward his new threat, Lou brought his rifle up and around, levered a cartridge into the chamber and fired. The rider had his rifle up to his shoulder as he sat on his horse.

Lou's shot entered the man's stomach. The man sat for a moment in the saddle then dropped his rifle. The horse squealed, sidestepped and reared high into the air. The rider fell sideways, his left foot caught in the stirrup. The horse ran, dragging the man, then reared up again, kicking and stomping to rid itself of what was hanging from its side.

Lou dragged himself through the snow to the nearest cover—a large boulder with a shrub oak tree and a clump of bear grass. His breath came heavily, and he could feel sweat running freely down his face and neck, the salt stinging his eyes. He reached in his back pocket, retrieved an old tattered blue handkerchief, wiped his eyes, then his face and neck. Once his vision was cleared, he reached into his jacket pocket where he kept extra rounds. He fully loaded the rifle, then reached for the .45 Colt revolver encased in the cross-draw leather holster at his belt on the left side. It was still there—a small comfort to the old cowman.

Using his belt knife, he cut his leather chaps and pant's leg at the left knee. *My Gawd ... whole knee's blowed away ... got... to stop the bleedin'.* He reached down and used the handkerchief as he best could as a bandage, but bright blood immediately saturated the cloth and dripped onto the snow. An artery severed? Exhaling, he pushed back thoughts of dread and death. He took three long breaths, holding each one a moment then exhaled slowly. Calmer now, he removed the belt from his britches and cinched above the knee until the flow of blood trickled to a stop.

"¿Qué pasa amigos? ¿Donde esta el Diablo?" The voice resounded through the canyon bottom. Lou heard cattle

milling around close by and movement from the general direction of the voice. The snow was coming down more rapidly now. As snow accumulated on his face and head, he wished he hadn't lost his hat earlier. The wet snow blew into his eyes, making his vision even more difficult. His left leg felt numb and cold. He scooped some snow into his mouth to help with the dryness and listened for any sound of movement.

The heavily accented voice spoke again. This time it came from a different direction. From the left now? "Hey, *Diablo.*"

Campbell made no effort to respond.

Again the voice ... this time from the right? "¡*Hombre Diablo*! Where are yew, gringo?" A pause.

"Yew haf keeled my horse and some of my men, gringo. Yew haf come from hell down on *me.*"

Another pause. Lou heard movement again from another direction beyond the wall of falling snow. Several moments passed. Lou heard whispering in Spanish and movement near where he lay. He made a mental effort to remember the location. He wiped snow from his eyes and his head, shook himself, and checked his rifle to ensure that the hammer was cocked with the chamber loaded. *They'll most likely try an' rush me if they kin figger out my position.* In the army they had called it probing for the enemy's location.

Just like when he and Elliott were in Cuba with the Rough Riders. His eyes felt heavy and he was very tired. Malaria, dengue fever, dysentery. Hardtack ... death ... so much death ...

From his position in the brush along the banks of the San Juan River in Cuba, Lou had watched as Elliott sprinted for cover a hundred yards away. *Ze-e-eu!* A bullet smacked into the tall grass a few feet from Elliott's last position. Lou strained his eyes to see the sniper's location. *Which tree, dammit?* The Spaniards were using smokeless powder—

wait ... there he is! He observed a patch of white within the confines of a tree. Bringing his Krag-Jorgensen rifle to bear on the newly acquired target, he took a deep breath with his finger on the trigger. *Thwa-a-ak!* A round hit near Elliott's head. Lou heard another bullet hit something—soft, like tissue? Elliott grunted and grasped his right knee with both hands. *Easy now, you ain't got no smokeless powder...got to take this sniper out quick.* Lou took another deep breath, held it while maintaining his sight picture and alignment, and slowly squeezed off the shot. The rifle bucked against his shoulder, and he watched the sniper fall from the tree. Elliott stood up awkwardly then stumbled forward. Lou heard a distinct pistol shot and knew his "huntin' pard" had finished the job.

It seemed so long ago that the two of them had left for Cuba aboard a transport ship with the Rough Riders on June 13, 1898. They had been part of a regiment of 1,000 men proud to serve their country and defeat the Spanish. He and Elliott had made it over with Troop A in the midst of heavy combat.

Lou smiled; he could still see Teddy Roosevelt at Kettle Hill initially charging the enemy at San Juan Heights with only five of 400 men. He and Elliott joined in the charge with the rest of the men when they finally figured out what ol' Teddy wanted. Marian had been so happy to see him come back all in one piece. She was a mighty fine woman. Yessir, she was that.

Footsteps scrunched in the snow close by. Straining to hear the slightest sound, Lou pushed the memories from his head and concentrated on the present. The rustlers were probing to determine his position alright. He could hear sound from at least three different locations, all out in front of him. None to his rear, though. That was a good thing. It was getting colder and the snow seemed to be lessening in its intensity. He dared not move; even the slightest move-ment such as brushing snow from his face might draw fire.

He inched the rifle up in front of him, ready to fire. Long moments passed. A figure moved toward him and then disappeared in the poor visibility. They were moving in his direction. Again ... there was the hat ... a black sombrero maybe? He brought the rifle to his shoulder and slowly pulled back on the trigger. *Blam*! The rifle shot surprised him, belching smoke and flame into the cold air. He quickly reloaded and fired another round closer to the ground this time in the same direction. A man screamed in pain, then nothing. He knew he should be moving. *Now*. But he couldn't.

Lou rolled slowly to his right. A volley riddled the air; the bullets whined and thudded into the ground where he had been lying. He wanted to cry out from the terrible pain in his knee, but he did not.

He thought briefly about his friend Domingo hoping that he was not dead, but he feared otherwise. Then he thought about his family—his wife Marian and their two children, Megan and Joaquin. If today was his time to die ... well, he had no regrets, none atall. *I love you Marian ... more'n ever I reckon...them kids a whole bunch too.*The snow had less-ened. Lou knew they would be on him soon with nowhere to run with his busted knee. No matter. He'd take out a few more rustlers and bandits before they got him. And Elliott—his friend wouldn't rest until everyone responsible was caught or dead.

He heard the same voice scream again from the right. "¡*Matenlo! ¡Matenlo*!" Lou turned and fired three rounds as quickly as he could reload and fire. Out of the corner of his eye, he saw forms moving. Coming right at him. He turned and fired the last round from the rifle at the figures running toward him. He heard the loud report of rifles and revolvers and felt bullets pass close to him and thud into the boulder and vegetation surrounding him, many ricocheting off into the snow.

Miraculously, he didn't feel any of the rounds hitting him. He drew his .45 Colt, cocked it, and fired at a man almost on top of him. The big gun boomed and bucked in his hand. The man screamed and reeled backward. Lou turned the gun to his right. *Come and git it, boys! This ol' cowpuncher ain't daid yet.*

He fired twice more. Then the bullets slammed hard into his body, taking his breath away. They felt like red-hot pokers slicing through the very core of his being. He fell violently back onto the snow, sighed deeply and was still.

Moments later, a man dressed in black, wearing a black sombrero, walked up and stood over him for several minutes. The man's right hand held a revolver. Blood ran down his shirtsleeve past the revolver, staining the snow red. The man spat a stream of dark brown tobacco juice.

"¡Indio! ¡Vamamos, Jefe!"

"Tenemos las bacas."

Indio Chacon stepped back and turned from the prostrate man lying in the snow. He thought it was good that he did not have to shoot the man again. The man, who ever he was, had *cojones*. That was for damn sure. In the old days, he would have cut the man's head off and taken it with him as a trophy. Respectfully, he looked down at the cowpuncher again. "*Hombre Diablo* ... yew haf cost me ... thees day."

CHAPTER TEN

F ather Ramon Quinones shuffled his sandaled feet through the dusty courtyard of San Xavier del Bac Mission south of the old pueblo, Tucson. The old Jesuit priest stopped just outside the shade of a large mesquite tree. He closed his eyes and raised his face to the sunshine. *Ahh ... I do love the sunshine and the warmth it provides.* To be outdoors, closer to his God; how many years now since he had worked with these wonderful Indians? He paused, absorbing the sunlight. Thirty years? Had life gone by so quickly? How he loved the southwest, its dryness and low humidity.

Father Ramon's eyes popped open. Was that a horse that he'd just heard stamp its foot on the compacted soil in front of the church? The priest cocked his head to listen. Yes. There is was again. *It isn't time for mass for a couple of hours. Who could it be at this early hour?* He strode out of the courtyard to the front of the mission, as quickly as his arthritic knees would allow. A gray gelding with black mane and tail stood at the hitch rack, his tail swishing back and forth keeping the flies away. The bay horse looked familiar and yet, he couldn't remember where he'd seen it before or who the owner might be.

He walked past the horse toward the entrance to the church, lifted his heavy robe slightly as he climbed the few steps up out of the sunshine into the church's interior. As his eyes adjusted to the dark interior, he heard the jingle of spurs rake the wooden floor behind him. As he turned toward the sound, a low, unassuming voice reached out to him.

"Howdy, padre. You're up an' at 'em early, ain't ya?"

Father Quinones could now see more clearly in the darkened interior. A man approached with his right hand outstretched, a battered Stetson hat in his left hand. He appeared to be white-headed with a similar colored mustache, and his clothing was dust-covered from his blue cotton shirt to his chaps and boots. The man was armed with two revolvers, one in a belt holster on the right side, the other in a leather shoulder holster snugged back under his left armpit.

"I'm sorry my son, but I do not allow guns in my church. Do I know you?" The priest accepted the warm, hardy handshake, his eyes drawn to the five-pointed silver star pinned to the man's shirt. The badge was inscribed with "Arizona Rangers" and the number "7" directly above it.

"*Lo siento mucho, padre.*" The man held his battered hat with both hands, looking down at the floor of the church and shuffled his boots, "These here pistols hafta stay with me. No harm intended." The man paused. "Reckon you an' me could mebbe step out and talk fer a spell?"

"Elliott? Is that you, my friend?" stammered the priest.

"Yessir, I reckon so," drawled the Ranger.

"Certainly, let's go outside ... into God's real world, *mi amigo.*"

The priest led the way out of the church, down the steps and to the courtyard to sit down on an old wooden bench under the shade of a large cottonwood tree. Father Quinones looked at the man sitting next to him. He saw the bright blue eyes, the tanned leathery face that had hardened over the years.

"My friend, how long has it been since you were last here—at the mission with me?"

Elliott sighed, looked off into the distance toward the Santa Rita Mountains to the southeast, "Pert near seven

... eight years, I reckon. It don't seem that long though."

"And you, my son—are you still praying to God?"

"Ever' *goddamn* day, padre."

The old priest flinched, cleared his throat, then replied evenly, "*Señor,* please do not use blasphemy."

Elliott's face reddened. "What I meant to say was thet I pray the old wooden rosary you gave me ever' day, an' I ask God to forgive me fer what I done."

Elliott leaned forward on the bench, rolling the hat between his hands, staring at the ground at his feet. He squinted as he clenched his teeth. "I'll do whatever it takes to be with her an' the boy one day ... *whatever it takes.*"

Father Quinones thought back to thirty some years ago, marrying this hard man to a gentle beautiful woman. They had all been young then and now—the woman was dead, the men were old, striving to be at peace with their God before it was their time to die.

He remembered Elliott and his bride of Spanish descent from Santa Fe. They had been so happy and the world so full of promise for them. "Do you want to confess your sins today, my friend?"

Elliott stirred. "I reckon so. I shore 'nough want to make it right with Gawd—so's I kin be with my wife an' boy in heaven when my time comes. You reckon He'll forgive me ... given all the turrible things I've done?"

Father Quinones answered, "God forgives anyone who's *truly* repentant."

"I am thet."

It was the priest's turn to pause. "Do you want to go inside—to the confessional, my son?"

Elliott looked him squarely in the eye. "Anything I got to say won't need to be behind no curtains, but face to face outside where the Gawd I know kin hear."

The priest listened patiently. Those piercing blue eyes

bored into his own as the man talked of death, hatred, bitterness, killings and mutilations, and more killings, bitterness. When Elliott finished speaking, Father Quinones knew in his heart that the man felt better for it.

"I will pray for you, *Señor* Elliott; you continue praying each day. God is listening, my friend."

Elliott placed his hat squarely on his head and reached for "makins" in his pocket. He built a cigarette, lit it, drew deeply and exhaled. "It ain't jest the killin', padre. All them woulda killed me if'n I hadn't done 'em in first. They was all bad men an' Injuns, but the cuttin' 'em up ... then hirin' my gun out. Why, thet was jest plumb wrong."

He looked off in the distance at the mountains again for a long time. The priest let him take his time, allowing him to sort out his thoughts. Father Quinones understood now why this good man had sinned. It was wrong to be sure, but yet—understandable. Obviously, the priest had no wife to compare, but he had a sister and a mother up until several years ago. If some evil person ever ... then who knows what a man's capable of?

Elliott interrupted his thoughts. "I shore hope I never hate like thet ever again, padre. When I kill a man now it's because I hafta as a lawman—when it's him or me an' he won't be hauled in to jail fer trial." He finished his cigarette and ground it out beneath his boot.

Father Quinones placed his hand on Elliott's shoulder and said softly, "I believe you are doing all you can. It's up to God now."

Elliott sighed deeply. "I reckon so. I can't go back in time and change things. Just got to do what's right from here on."

"Thank God we have men like you to protect us, Elliott."

The man gazed at the priest, his blue eyes squinting in the bright sunlight, his lips pursed. "I ain't been the best Catholic, padre ... not like mah wife. She was the *real* thing,

I reckon. Church ever' Sunday, rain or shine." He stood up and shook some of the dust off his clothes. "I do believe in God though, padre. Honest Injun, *I do thet.* Can't help but feel Him ever' day ... mostly when I'm outdoors."

"You are a good man, Elliott, and a good Christian. Someday, I hope that you will be a good Catholic like your wife was, *Señor.* But for now—to be what you are is all that God wants. I will pray that you will be at peace with that for now, my friend."

Elliott extended his hand. "One of these days, padre, if'n I live long enough, the killin' will stop fer me, an' I'll put these here *pistolas* up fer good." Then he strode to the horse standing impatiently at the hitch rack, untied the reins and swung easily up in the saddle. "God willin', padre. "¡*Hasta luego!*"

"We will meet again, my friend, this I know ... either here on earth or ... perhaps ..."

The dusty old Ranger did not hear the priest as he headed south at a trot. He had some hard miles to put in and little daylight left.

CHAPTER ELEVEN

Megan Campbell swung the heavy axe in her tired arms. It came down hard, splitting the bolt of wood that she had placed up on the worn chopping block. Awakening early, she had roused her son, dressed and ate a meager breakfast. She finished splitting wood for the schoolhouse. Later, after school she would split more wood for her residence that was located behind and adjacent to the schoolhouse; there was no time now. The children would be coming soon. It had been a dreary, difficult winter with an abundance of snow and bitter cold. Shivering, she looked up at the sky then piled a load of split wood in her arms. It was cold and uncomfortable in the one-room schoolhouse without a warm fire in the potbelly wood stove. She carried the last of the split wood inside the schoolhouse, piled it in the wood box next to the stove then laid kindling on top of paper that she had placed inside the stove on top of cold, gray ashes from the previous day's fire. *Thank God, I kept some dry kindling in out of the snow and wet.* She struck a match, lit the paper, and blew softly, fanning the delicate flames. She watched anxiously as the kindling began to slowly catch fire. *Come on—come on ...burn.* Once the kindling was burning well, she added larger chucks of wood and soon had a roaring fire going in the stove.

The children arrived a short time later, and class began. The day progressed into the afternoon, and before she knew it, the school day was almost over. Using the chalkboard, Megan wrote down the homework assignments for

each class, anticipating their groans. The kids hated homework as much as she disliked having to grade all the papers.
All the children had work and chores when they returned
home after school and homework would be done only after
the ranch work was completed. She shook her head. *But
they need the extra work to learn as much as possible before leaving
school for good.*

She had twelve white children to teach each day at the
school, from first grade all the way up to the eighth grade,
creating a nightmare teaching all the various levels in the
same room. Megan sighed. *Is it all worth it?* But she had
known the circumstances going into the teaching job many
years ago. *It's what I want to do.*

On Saturdays, she taught several of the Mexican children from the community. It was not much, but it *was* something. She had fought hard with the school board to achieve
even that victory. They finally agreed with her as long as she
did not receive any additional salary—and the White and
Mexican children were not taught together.

She heard a squeal from the rear of the room and turned
quickly from the chalkboard to see one of the boys pulling
both pigtails on the girl seated in front of him.

"Billy Joe, you stop that! I mean *right now!*"

The boy caught in the act, let go of the pigtails and
jumped backward in his wooden desk away from the girl in
front of him. Embarrassed, his face turned red.

"I didn't mean nothin', Miz Campbell ... just funnin'
some with Sue is all."

"You didn't mean *anything*, Billy Joe. Don't be using double negatives. This is English, not Spanish we're speaking
at the moment, and you know better than to be touching
another student in class ... much less pulling someone's
hair." She looked steadily at him knowing he was not a
mean person.

"Yes ma'am."

"If it happens again, you'll be sitting in the corner of the room for the rest of the day. What's more, I'll have a talk with your father." She walked over to his desk. "And you know what that will mean ... don't you Billy Joe?"

"Yes ma'am. I reckon it won't happen again."

She walked back to the front of the classroom and addressed all the students. "That's all for today. Make sure you write down your homework assignments and have your work done to turn in first thing tomorrow morning. If you older students could help your younger brothers and sisters with getting the assignments written down for them, I would appreciate it."

She moved closer to the children, smiled at them. "Thank you for a good day. Be careful going home, and I will see you tomorrow."

The children rushed toward the coatroom, stumbling over each other, squealing, laughing. One by one, they exited the little schoolhouse in their excitement to get home.

Her son Tim stood up from his assigned desk, grasped his homemade wooden crutches and walked slowly to the front of the room. "You want me to help clean the chalkboard, Mom?"

"Sure Tim. That would be a big help. Thank you."

She watched her ten year old son walk with difficulty to the chalkboard. His right foot turned in slightly, and it was difficult to stand on his right leg from the polio eight years ago. Oh, she had been so scared. The high fever, the paralysis, the difficulty in breathing. Tim had almost died, but somehow, someway, he had been allowed to live. Several others in the neighborhood had died from polio that year.

At the time, Megan didn't think he'd ever walk again, but she was just happy to have him alive. She watched him lean one crutch against the wall—the crutches Papa had made him. Tears welled in her eyes, she turned to brush them aside, remembering her son's struggle to learn to walk. *He's done so well. I am so proud of him.*

Tim braced his left hand on the eraser shelf under the chalkboard, then placed the second crutch next to the first, and began erasing the assignments from the board.

As Megan leaned over her desk, placing papers into a bag, she thought she heard something outside the schoolhouse. She listened for a moment, straining to hear. Spurs clinked faintly outside near the woodpile. Frowning, she went to the door and looked outside. The day was still dreary looking, windy, and overcast with gray skies. She thought maybe it would snow again or at least rain or hail. She opened the door fully and stepped outside on the open porch, feeling the cold air, and looked toward the woodpile.

"Wel-l-l, if it ain't thet purty schoolmarm I heerd tell of ..."

Then she saw Elliott standing near the woodpile with an armload of chopped wood. He started toward her, his spurs clinking musically. His blue eyes twinkled and a smile broke out on his tanned, leathery face.

"Elliott! What are you doing here? I had no idea you were coming." She unconsciously brushed back the hair from her face and straightened her dress.

He strode up the steps and as he passed her, he winked. "I'll jest put this here wood by the stove fer ya, *'lil missy.*"

She followed him in, closed the door to the outside cold, and stood back while he placed the wood near the stove. He turned, held out his arms and embraced her. *He feels so good—so strong.* Megan's face flushed.

An eraser thumped onto the floor. Elliott turned toward her son at the chalkboard. "Howdy, Timmy. She got ya working after school fer her, boy?"

"Yes sir. I kinda asked if I could help."

"Good lad! Thet's the idée, son. Help your mom all ya kin."

Megan smiled at Elliott, said nothing, but tucked her head against his chest and hugged him again, and then again—always so glad to see him.

He laughed heartily, held her out away from him by her shoulders, looking her up and down. "Megan darlin', you're shore the best lookin' woman ... *ever*."

She looked down from those piercing blue eyes and bit at her lower lip. "Where have ... what have you been doing, Elliott? We haven't seen you ... since ... the Christmas dance, right?"

Releasing her shoulders, he opened the heavy door to the stove and placed more wood on the fire. He removed his gloves and opened the heavy mackinaw jacket. Then he stood with his back to the wood stove that radiated heat into the room.

"I reckon thet's about right, Meg. How you two been doin'?"

"Oh, we're fine. Thanks. How about you?"

"I'm plumb wore down to the nub today; thet's fer shore. We was chasing rustlers up in the Rincons. I swung on down by San Xavier Mission early this morning then over the Santa Ritas and down to here." Elliott rubbed his hands over the fire. "It's been a long day, Meg. If'n it's all right with you, I'll bed down here in the schoolhouse tonight then head over to your folk's place tomorrow morning. Looks like there's a storm brewing out yonder; I'd jest as soon hit thet nine-mile ride *manana*." He paused. "Will them loose-tongued gossipers give you a hard time with me stayin' in the schoolhouse?"

"Of course you can stay over, Elliott. I don't pay much attention to gossip. And Timmy and I will have a chance to talk to you tonight. Put Viento in the corral and bring your bedroll in here. We were going to have some stew for supper. Would you care to join us?"

"It would be mah pleasure, ma'am!" He bowed and took off his hat, sweeping it in a wide arc.

Megan laughed at his silliness. He looked older than she last recalled. His hair was almost completely white. What had happened to all the black and gray? She chuckled to herself. *Well, I'm no spring chicken myself.* Her father had told her and Joaquin a long time ago that life flew by quickly, and everyone should make the most out of every day.

"You get your horse and gear squared away then come on around to our place. I'll have us some supper to eat just as soon as I can get it together."

"It's a deal. I'll split some more wood and kindling and bring it inside fer the hot meal ... an' much obliged, Meg." He looked over at Timmy. "You want to come an' help me with Viento? He's been wantin' to see ya."

"*Could I,* Elliott? Can I sit on him ... do you think?"

"Yessir ... I reckon so. Ol' Viento, why he'd be mighty proud if you'd do 'im the honors."

The boy looked at his mother for approval.

"Yes, of course you can, Timmy. You help Elliott then come on in to the house. Put your coat on before going outside, young man."

The old Ranger and the young boy walked out of the schoolhouse slowly down the steps, the boy insisting on doing it on his own without any assistance. Then they walked to the horse tied to the hitch post.

"Viento, amigo! You recollect this here strong lad, huh?" Elliott patted the horse's neck affectionately. The horse appeared to study the boy standing beside his master. Only then did he whinny and nod his head as if to say,

"Howdy friend!"

Elliott laughed out loud. "You wanna climb aboard?" The boy nodded. He dropped his crutches and Elliott swung him up in the saddle, handing him the reins.

"Now remember, Timmy ... keep the slack outta them reins, but not too tight. Use your knees to hang on, an' if need be, grab aholt of thet saddle horn."

The horse broke into a light trot with the boy laughing and enjoying the ride, the independence and confidence that had been instilled within him.

"Thet's the ticket. Ya got ol' Viento buffaloed fer shore. We'll make a cowpuncher out of ya yet."

The horse stopped next to Elliott and nudged his shoulder. Elliott lifted the boy off the horse. Timmy stood; hanging on to the stirrup, and Elliott picked up the crutches and handed them to him.

"Gee ... thanks, Elliott. That was a lot of fun. Can I ride him again sometime?"

Elliott walked toward the corral, leading the horse, and the boy followed slowly on his crutches. "I reckon you kin ride ol' Viento anytime you want, Tim. I'm thinkin' he likes you a lot. I shore 'nough do."

He unsaddled the horse, rubbed him down and curry-combed his back. He made sure the horse had water and fed him hay with the two horses that Megan had in the corral. Viento trotted around the corral with the other horses like it was old home week. Elliott picked up his saddle and bedroll and headed for the schoolhouse. He turned to the boy and said, "I'll stash this gear inside. Have a seat on the steps. I'll be right back."

When he came back, he sat down beside Timmy. Elliott reached over and put his arm around the boy's shoulder.

"I missed ya, Timmy. Don't get to see ya 'nough, I reckon."

"I miss you too, Elliott." Timmy shuffled the crutches he held between his legs. "You sure have been awful good to me and my mom." He looked out over the bleak desert landscape. "I ... both of us owe you an awful lot. We ..."

"Naw, you don't owe me nothin' atall. Your dad would've done the same fer me, I reckon."

"What really happened to my dad? My mom said he was a brave man—like you."

Elliott paused. "He was a real hero, Timmy. You kin be real proud of 'im." *No point in tellin' the boy thet his daddy tripped tryin' to git off the train thet was bein' robbed. Tripped and was shot down by no good, murderin' sumbitches.*

"Elliott, do you ... what I mean to say is ... well ..."

"Spit it out, son. Don't be lollygaggin' with me. "

"Do you ...uh ... *like* me?"

Elliott hugged him. "I reckon I do at thet. I love ya like ya was my own son. You're extree special to me an' don't ya ever forgit it."

"You too, Elliott! I wish you were my dad. I wish so much ... that I even had a dad." Timmy sighed. His face downcast, sad, his eyes welled with tears.

"Wel-l-l now, I'm mighty proud that you would think so highly o' me. Why don't you jest think of me bein' your Dad from now on. You know ... our 'lil secret. No need to share with your mom or anyone else, right?

"*Yes sir.* Our secret, Elliott ... just you and me." His face brightened, his eyes widened, and he smiled broadly. Then his expression turned serious. "You know sometimes ... I get to feeling bad about ... about myself being crippled and all."

He hesitated, Elliott said nothing. Timmy pursed his lips, "I mean—will I ever amount to anything, Elliott? What can I do with my life? I don't want my mom to take care of me all my life."

Elliott waited to see if the boy had more to say, and

seeing that he didn't, he asked, "How old are ya now, Timmy?"

He drew himself up taller. "I'm ten years old this year."

"I woulda figgered older ... with you being so growed up lookin' an' all." He allowed the boy to take in what he had just said. "Well, no matter, boy. The thing is ... as I see it, you kin let thet leg and foot keep ya from gittin' what ya want in life or you kin make somethin' outta yerself. You're always goin' to have thet bum leg and foot I reckon, so you ain't goin' to be no cowpuncher or ranger."

He reached in his shirt pocket for his tobacco and papers then he searched in his jacket pocket. Upon finding his "makins," he rolled his cigarette, lit it, and drew on the cigarette calmly while studying the glowing end.

Elliott continued. "Way I see it son, it's a blessing fer ya in someways. Why, the life of a cowpuncher or ranger ain't the best by any means. On the other hand, if ya was to be a schoolteacher like your mom or a storekeeper or sech, why you'd make out better in the long run. You need to git thet learnin' from school. Then go on to the school in Tucson thet your mom went to. I'd say thet's the ticket fer ya, son."

"I get so tired of people staring at me all the time. I just want to fit in. You know, like everybody else."

"I'd say your fittin' in right well ... thet is, with them thet counts. As fer people staring, there's no excuse fer it. Jest pure ig-ne-rence, I'd say. Don't pay them people no never mind. They ain't worth your time spent worrin' over 'em."

Elliott stood up, stretched out his sore knee, and tossed the cigarette butt to the ground. "We'd best be gettin' in fer supper 'afore your mom comes lookin' fer us, Timmy."

The Ranger looked down at the boy seated on the steps, then out toward the Whetstone Mountains to the east with Biscuit Mountain's bald round top prominent in the forefront of the mountain range separating them from Fort Huachuca.

"You be who ya are, Timmy, an' you'll do jest fine in life."

"Thanks for talking to me and being my dad, Elliott. Don't you worry, I can keep a secret," whispered Timmy.

They walked together around the schoolhouse to the living quarters in back. All of them sat down to eat and were just finishing supper when they heard hooves pounding. Elliott slipped out the door, away from the well-lit house and peered into the darkness. He could make out a horse and a rider racing toward them. *What the heck?*

The horse slid to a stop in front of the house, its rider slipping to the ground before the horse came to a complete stop. "Megan! Megan! It's me ... Joaquin! Come quick!"

Elliott stepped from the inky darkness out into the light. "What's wrong, boy?"

Joaquin stopped running. "Elliott? Is that you?" His breath was ragged. "Thank God—it *is* you! Where's Megan?"

"*Calmaté, mi'jo.* Jest hold your hosses!"

"It's Dad ... he's been shot! He's dead and Domingo's hurt real bad!"

CHAPTER TWELVE

"**W**ould anyone like to say a few words for the deceased ... Lou Campbell?"

His blue eyes squinting, Elliott watched Father Quinones clutch his bible firmly and step closer to the grave. The old priest nervously cleared his throat, looked at the Campbell family and friends gathered across from him. They all stood under the big cottonwood tree down a ways from the ranch house. Father Quinones' robe fluttered in the breeze. It was a cool breezy day, not bitter cold, and the sky clear blue with warm sunshine allowing some respite from the waning days of winter.

It was mighty quiet, Elliott thought. Ever' body cryin' or quiet-like, not polite talk 'bout ranchin', the weather, or even a howdy-do—jest silence, thet an' the wind. Well, it shore ain't a good day fer none of us. Thet damned Chacon. Damn his murderin' hide. Ain't nobody wants to talk now. I kin damn well understand thet ... might break down in front o' these good folks. Somebody's gotta say—somethin' though, I reckon.

Holding his Stetson in his hands, Elliott stepped cautiously forward from between Marian and Megan Campbell. With a sigh, he looked down at the wooden casket he had built the day before, placing his long-time friend in it that morning. Joaquin and he had spent hours digging the grave the previous day.

He started to speak, took a deep breath, swallowed hard, and began again, "Gawd, I reckon I palaver with ya most ever day 'bout me ... an' what I'm always wantin'. Well, today I ain't askin' fer me, but fer mah good friend here. I've knowed Lou fer a long while, an' he's been the finest man I reckon I ever knowed in mah lifetime." Elliott swallowed past the lump in his throat. "He was a true friend, a good man an' father, husband to Marian here. He was one of the best cowmen thet's ever set a hoss."

Elliott glanced over at Marian and Megan, who were hugging each other and sobbing. Joaquin stood with a deep sadness written on his face. Elliott's jaw tightened as he looked up into the bright, blue skies. "What I mean is ... he *de*-serves the good life up there in heaven. He's paid more'n his dues down here." He shuffled his boots. "Now, I don't reckon he'll be needin' any mah good credit, thet is if'n I have any. But if'n he does ... why, you give 'im mah share an' make sure he gets the best up yonder."

Elliott turned away from the grave and walked back to stand next to Joaquin and Tim. At Father Quinones' direction, they lowered the coffin into the grave. While the mourners returned to the ranch house, Elliott and Joaquin remained to fill in the grave they'd spent hours digging the day before.

Both men worked tirelessly throwing shovel full after shovel full of dirt on top of the wooden coffin. Neither spoke, determined to remain engrossed in the task at hand, working as hard as possible to get it done. A few light clouds drifted slowly by, the wind picked up, cooling them.

Joaquin stopped shoveling dirt, removed the blue bandana around his neck, and wiped the perspiration from his face. He cleared his throat. "I want to join the Rangers, Elliott."

Elliott stopped shoveling. "You *what?*"

"You heard me, dammit!"

Elliott jabbed his shovel into the loose pile of dirt next

to the grave, rested his foot on the shovel blade, his hands on the handle. He leaned slightly forward. "You use thet tone of voice with me agin', boy, I'll tan your hide then I'll wash your mouth out with soap fer swearin'."

"Aw ... Elliott, I'm sorry for talkin' to you that way. It's just that with my Dad gone now ... well, I figger to track down and kill that son-of-a-bitch Chacon. I won't rest till I get the job done."

"Been a lotta good men try to take 'im afore you; ain't none o' 'em thet I know of got the job done."

"I don't give a damn, Elliott. If he kills me ... so be it, but I want him bad—*real bad.*" Joaquin gritted his teeth and a seething hatred exuded from his very being.

"Last time I checked, Rangers ain't in the habit of murderin' people fer any reason, *mi'jo.* Ya do thet an' you're jest as bad as Chacon."

"What do you know about it anyways?" Joaquin's face reddened, eyes pointed. "My dad means something to *me*... even if he doesn't to you!"

Elliott narrowed his eyes as if to pierce the very core of the young man standing across from him. His voice had a hard edge. "Your dad was the finest man I ever knowed an' rode with. You ever say somethin' like thet agin—I'll knock your head plumb off!" He turned and looked south toward Mexico for a few moments. "You leave Chacon to me an' the Rangers. We'll bring 'im in. He'll stand trial an' be hung when he's found guilty o' murderin' Bob Williams an' your dad."

"No! I want to go with you, Elliott."

"So's ya kin gun 'im down, eh?"

Joaquin dropped his shovel and stepped forward. "Sure, I admit that I'd like to do that right here ... right now, and not feel bad about it, not one bit. But if you say no, then I'll do it your way. You got my word on it, Elliott."

Elliott stepped back from the grave, sighed and ran his hand over his face. His eyes closed for a moment. "They've not filled Ayala's Ranger job yet thet I know of. 'Course you'll most likely be needed on the ranch helpin' your mom an' Domingo out ...?"

Joaquin's face brightened. "Carmen said she'd be willin' to do more to help out, and I can come home and work the spring roundup can't I?"

"Carmen willin' fer ya to be a lawman, is she?"

"She wants me to do what's right. She feels like I do. We're sick and tired of bad men and outlaws like Chacon doing as they please in the territory—murdering honest folk, rustling cattle, robbing trains and the like. They need to be stopped, Elliott, and I can help."

"I reckon ya might sign on fer a year, boy, an' see if'n it worked out fer ya." Elliott paused. "It's a hard life an' one like as not will git ya killed. What do ya think your dad would say 'bout all this, *mi'jo?*"

Joaquin sat down on the dirt pile and tipped his hat back on his head. "I reckon he'd say it was my call. And whatever I decided, to not go about it halfcocked. To think it through and then get the job done right."

Elliott stepped back to his shovel and picked it up. "I'll finish up here. You best go on in an' talk to your mom 'bout becomin' a lawman. Then we'll see, boy. I reckon we'll see."

Joaquin strode toward the ranch house, a frown on his dark face.

"Hey ... *mi'jo!*"

Joaquin stopped and turned back toward the gravesite.

Elliott continued, "I'll be needin' your word right here an' now thet ya'll do things my way with Chacon."

"Sure." Joaquin looked steadily into the old Ranger's eyes. "You have my word on it."

"We'll bring 'im in—if'n we kin, an' when he's found

guilty we'll watch him swing fer what he's done. No shootin'
'im down in cold blood."

"No sir, however you say, Elliott."

"And another thing ... I don't want to see no hateful bitterness eatin' ya up from here on. *You understand me, boy.*"

"Yessir."

"You *damn* well better! I know what the hell I'm talkin'
'bout. I spent most of the prime time of mah life doin'
jest thet when mah wife and boy was killed. It'll eat ya up
inside an' wear ya plumb down to the nub. Worse, it kin
make a killer outta ya. Then you ain't no better'n them
you're chasing down."

Joaquin started to reply, chose not to, his face sad,
pensive.

Elliott waved a backhand toward the ranch house. "You
go on now. Talk to your family." Joaquin turned and walked
toward the ranch house.

Elliott bent down and picked up the shovel, his thoughts
elsewhere in a time long ago. *Damn, it's been a long while—
feelin' this away.* He was a young man once. Yessir, he had
the bull by the horns in them days. He was married to the
purtiest gal in the territory. He and Maria had a son. They
named him Joaquin. A good wife ... a fine son to be proud
of ...all gone now fer a long while. He brushed a tear away.

What had happened to all them years since? Wasted
away? Gawd almighty, but the years fly by, don't they, hoss?
Whatever ya do, don't let Joaquin become like you. Try an' be
a good example fer 'im. Maria would want thet, I reckon.

Elliott worked at filling the grave, sweating in the cool-
ness of the morning. *I'll pray thet rosary ever' day ...like I promised. And you help me with mah temper an' killin' ways. Thet an'
keepin' the boy safe.* He sighed deeply and looked up into the
heavens. *It ain't askin' too much of an old man—is it?*

CHAPTER THIRTEEN
Spring, 1904

J oaquin stepped down off the train in Phoenix with his valise. Elliott was visiting with the train's conductor. Unsure of his surroundings in the bustling city, Joaquin stood waiting anxiously for the old Ranger. The spring weather was nice and comfortable, not hot and miserable as he remembered his last visit with Elliott and his father the previous summer. He recalled the intense heat and humidity with the monsoon in full effect. They'd stayed at the Adams Hotel. The rooms were elegant, and they had slept out on the balcony as it was too hot inside the room. After checking for bed bugs and finding none, they had pushed the beds out onto the balcony for a good night's sleep.

Men on horseback rode up and down the dusty street with an occasional wagon rumbling by or a horse and buggy clipping along the street. Someone yelled, "*Watch out*! You damn fool."

Joaquin jumped aside as a young man sped by on a bicycle. He clutched his valise tightly and saw Elliott step down from the train. As they walked together along Washington Street past Second Avenue toward the Adams Hotel, Joaquin peered up at the electric lines and tall wooden poles supporting them. He stepped squarely into a pile of fresh horse manure where someone had previously parked a buggy.

"Shit!" He looked down at the mess on his boot.

Elliott guffawed. "It shore is ... big city got ya rattled, *mijo?*"

"Yes sir."

"Don't you be worryin' none 'bout thet horse dung on your boot. Why, my ol' man used to tell me thet the more manure a man had on his boots, the more credit he'd have at the bank."

Joaquin stopped in the street, gawking at two pretty young women wearing long dresses and hats. As they strolled by, they smiled shyly at him; one of them carried an umbrella for protection from the sun. Six or seven bicycles lay near the board sidewalk in front of The Boston Store with three horses and buggies tied up out front. His eyes wandered to the store adjacent to The Boston Store and read its sign "M. Goldwater & Bro Suit Cloak Annex." Most folks living in Phoenix seemed to walk, ride bicycles, or use the three crowded trolleys available from First Avenue and Washington Street running west to the capitol at Nineteenth Avenue. Elliott advised him town folks didn't want the chore of taking care of horses even if they could afford the cost of a horse and buggy.

Elliott and Joaquin walked west along Washington Street, passing First Avenue and the B. Heyman Furniture Co. Store. Many of the stores and hotels had awnings and porches over the windows and doorways. Several electric trolleys with "Phoenix Park and Capitol Grounds" passed by on the dusty street, all loaded to full capacity. Joaquin's father had told him the original trolleys in Phoenix were pulled by horses until 1897, when electricity became available in the city.

"Elliott, how many people you reckon live here ... in the city?"

"Why, I don't rightly know fer shore, *mijo*. I heerd tell o'er five thousand when they took the census count 'bout three year ago."

"Good Lord! That many?"

"Yessir ... I reckon so," drawled Elliott.

They saw the large, elegant Adams Hotel just down the street to the north of Washington Street.

Elliott stopped, pointing. "This here *ho*-tel is the meetin' place o' the movers an' shakers o' the territory, boy. All them big-shot politicians stay here when conductin' business at the capitol ... blowin' hot air mostly, I reckon." He took off his hat, scratched his head. "Anyhow, it was in this here *ho*-tel where ol' Burt Mossman agreed to be the first captain of the Arizona Rangers 'bout two years back, in March, 1901.

"Is he still captain? Asked Joaquin.

"I reckon not, *mi'jo*. He stepped down 'bout a year ago an' the Governor appointed Tom Rynning as the head honcho fer us."

Joaquin and Elliott stepped up on the sidewalk at the entrance to the Adams Hotel at the corner of Adams Street and Central Avenue. Joaquin marveled at the unique craftsmanship. A breath-taking, four-story hotel, it had balconies encompassing the hotel on each story and a single chimney strikingly poised at the top of the building.

When they walked into the lobby, Joaquin gaped at the beautiful furnishings and wonderful craftsmanship of the interior. "Wow. This is *some* hotel, Elliott."

They checked into a shared room for $1.50 a night, left their valises in the room, ventured back out to Washington Street, and waited on a trolley to take them to the capitol. Elliott was to meet Governor Alexander Brodie, Captain Tom Rynning and newly appointed Lieutenant Harry Wheeler at the new capitol building. Further, he had been ordered to bring Joaquin Campbell along with him to discuss the possibility of hiring him as a Ranger.

A trolley car stopped, Joaquin followed Elliott onto the car and gave the conductor the five-cent fare to ride twenty blocks to the capitol. They settled in the only available seating, directly behind two ladies who were sitting in the front seat near the conductor.

As the trolley traveled westward down Washington Street for several blocks, one of the ladies sniffed loudly, wiggling her nose, looking all around the trolley car. She was attired in a white blouse buttoned up to the nape of her neck, and a long, full-length brown skirt that mostly covered her black-laced shoes. A large hat, tied with a silk scarf around her pale face, topped the outfit. Her friend was dressed similarly, and it was obvious to Joaquin that both were wealthy, high society ladies.

The first woman continued the loud sniffing and said, "My goodness, Martha. Such an *offensive* odor!"

The other woman held her nose between her thumb and forefinger and agreed loudly. "A *stench,* my dear ... what on earth?"

Joaquin looked down at his boot. His face flushed. *Oh no, I still have horse manure on my boot.*

Elliott removed his hat and leaned forward between the two women. "Excoose me, ma'am," he directed at the first lady.

She turned toward him sharply in an annoyed manner. "*Yes?*"

"Wel-l-l ... ma'am ... I reckon you're right 'bout thet there odor. I mean it shore is *o*-fen-sive an' all." He pursed his lips while squinting his eyes as he leaned even closer to both women and in a very confidential manner continued, "Ma'am, the way I figger it ... it was the conductor who went an' broke wind. He does it again ... why, me and young Joaquin—we'll throw him an' his foul smell plumb off this here trolley!"

Both women reddened and turned away from Elliott.

"*Well!*" huffed the first woman.

Elliott settled back in his seat and folded his arms across his chest. Joaquin thought he might have seen the old Ranger's blue eyes twinkle just before he tipped his battered hat down over his face. As the trolley approached the capitol, no further conversation came from the fine ladies in the front seat.

They found their way up to the second-floor and looked for Governor Brodie's office. As they walked down the hallway, Elliott said, "This here capitol building was dedicated in February, 1901, *mi'jo*. Purty fancy, ain't it?"

The building and furnishings were so awesome, Joaquin couldn't reply. His mouth hung open. The Governor's secretary, a very serious young man wearing a suit and tie, showed them in to the office. As the door swung open, a man who appeared to be about Elliott's age strode toward them, his hand held out. Dressed elegantly in a dark suit and tie, he wore glasses and sported a large gray mustache. Joaquin couldn't help but stare—the man was missing one arm.

"Elliott, *amigo*! It's been awhile, my friend." They shook hands warmly, and the man turned to Joaquin, "And ... this is Lou's boy?"

"Shore is, Governor. This here's Joaquin."

Governor Brodie smiled broadly at Joaquin. "It's a pleasure, son. I knew your father well. He served under me in the Spanish-American War—a fine soldier and man." He hesitated. "I'm so sorry to hear about his death. Please relate my condolences to your family."

"Thank you. It's a pleasure to meet you, sir."

"Come in ... come in." Brodie motioned with his one arm for them to come into his office and have a seat. In the office sat two other men—one maybe six feet tall and thin with a large brown mustache, the other short and slender. Both stood and greeted the new arrivals.

"How are you, Elliott?" asked the tall man.

"Why, I reckon I'm fine an' fit as a fiddle, Tom. How are ya doin'?"

The tall man shook Elliott's hand and gestured toward the second man. "I asked Harry to come over as well."

Elliott smiled, shook the shorter man's hand. "It's always good to see you, Harry. Are ya still mah *Jefe?* I heerd thet ya was promoted to Lieutenant."

Joaquin stood, feeling uncomfortable in the company of men he did not know. *The legendary Harry Wheeler! And the tall man must be Captain Tom Rynning.*

Wheeler looked over at Captain Rynning. "That's part of what we need to discuss, Elliott." He turned to Joaquin. "Glad to meet you, Joaquin. The name's Wheeler. This is Captain Tom Rynning." He shook Joaquin's hand and motioned toward two chairs near the governor's desk. Governor Brodie sat behind his desk, retrieved a Cuban cigar box from the top of his desk, and offered one to each of the men. All accepted except Joaquin.

"No thank you, sir. I don't smoke."

"Good boy. It's a bad habit to take up." Brodie looked over at Rynning. "Now Tom, what are your plans to capture this Chacon fellow?"

Rynning leaned forward in his chair as he blew a cloud of cigar smoke up toward the ceiling of the huge room. "We'll find the son-of-a-bitch and bring him in—alive or dead, if need be, sir."

Wheeler gestured with his cigar. "Elliott?"

"I reckon Chacon is down in Mexico. He won't be movin' fer a spell ... jest layin' low till things blow over."

"Where in Mexico?" asked Governor Brodie.

"I expect he'll be at one o' them *rancherias* thet Cochise used in the Sierra Madres back in the ol' days, sir. I figger I know which one."

Wheeler spoke up, "How can you be certain, Elliott?"

"I've been there." Elliott shuffled uncomfortably in his chair and puffed on the cigar. "As a young feller, I worked as a scout fer the Army. I tracked Apaches down there many a time." His eyes hardened. "Never brought many o' 'em back as prisoner's thet I recall."

Brodie asked, "You think you can find him then ... bring him in?"

"Yessir ... I reckon so," the old Ranger drawled.

Brodie puffed on his cigar, his eyes wide. "Well gentlemen, let's go get him then ... *straight away!*"

It was Rynning's turn to shuffle uncomfortably in his chair. "There's the matter of dealing with the Mexican government, sir. You know—conducting law enforcement duties on foreign soil. They don't particularly like us going down there ... for any reason."

Wheeler looked at Rynning and said, "How's our relationship with the Sonoran Governor and the Rurales, Tom?"

"Currently, they're very good, Harry. I've been dealing with Colonel Kosterlitzky, the head of the Mexican Rurales. He's been most helpful. The problem with the Rurales is they tend to ... shoot most of their prisoners. Not many are captured and brought in for trial."

Wheeler continued, "You think you can work out a deal with the Governor and the Colonel for us to send a small Ranger force down there to get Chacon?"

"I can try. If they allow us down there, they'll want some Rurales riding with us," replied Rynning.

Wheeler looked at Elliott. "How many Rangers will you need to go down into Mexico? That is, if they even let us go ahead with this?"

"I figger a squad—maybe six men an' another two to four Rurales. We'll want to travel light and fast." Elliott puffed on the big cigar. "Four pack animals ought to do it fer supplies."

Wheeler interjected, "Which brings us to another matter that we need resolved. Elliott, we want you to take my old sergeant's position. You can take charge of the squad based out of the Ranger's office in Douglas."

The old Ranger chewed on a corner of his mustache. "Ya know, I ain't much fer ramrodin' a bunch o' men, Harry."

Joaquin leaned forward in his seat, squeezing his knees with both hands. He thought, yes! *Do it, Elliott. You're the best man for the job.*

Rynning stood up. "You'd be a snap for the job, Elliott, and I'm sure you can use the extra money—$10.00 more a month for you." He walked over to the window, looking out into the street below. "If you take the sergeant's job, we'll hire young Joaquin in Ayala's position. He can ride with your squad. How's that sound?"

"You shore know how to sweeten the pot, Tom ... I dunno ..."

Rynning turned from the window, walked to Joaquin. "You want to be a Ranger, son?"

"Yes sir."

"Well then, talk to this old bastard. Tell him he needs to take a little responsibility for someone other than himself once in awhile. As for you, you'll make $100 a month as a private—not bad wages, son. Hell, cowpunchers are paid $30 a month. Course they don't usually get shot at." Joaquin started to respond. "There's promotion in line for a good man, too. Captain's salary is $175 a month, Lieutenant's $130 a month, and as I said Sergeant's $110 a month ... a good career for the right man."

Before Joaquin could reply, Elliott asked Wheeler, "Is Bill Wade still on your old squad stationed in Douglas?"

"Why, yes he is. Do you have issues with him?" returned Wheeler.

"I reckon not much—aside from him bein' a jackass an'

treatin' Mexicans rough when it ain't needed."

"I've talked to him about being rough on prisoners. Apart from that, he's been a good Ranger and served us well."

"Wel-l-l, Tom, you're a hard man to say no to—I reckon I'll do it an' be proud to at thet."

"Excellent!" Rynning pulled several papers out of his saddlebags. "We'll sign you on first, young man. No time like the present. Governor, do you want to swear him in?"

"It would be my pleasure, Captain." Brodie stood, walked around the desk, and Rynning handed him the enlistment papers. "Stand up, son, and raise your right hand." Joaquin complied. "Do you swear to uphold the Constitution of the United States of America and the laws of the Territory of Arizona ... so help you, God?"

"Yes sir. I do"

"*Bueno*. Have a seat; read and sign your one-year enlistment paper."

Joaquin read the one-page document, placed his signature at the bottom of the page. His heart pounded in his chest. *Well, you've done it now, haven't you? No backing out ... stop it! You owe it to Dad to catch that son-of-a-bitch Chacon. And help bring law and order to the Arizona Territory.*

"You're officially an Arizona Ranger now, son," Brodie said smiling. Joaquin returned a weak smile.

Wheeler turned to Elliott. "What about training for Joaquin? I want some decent training for him before he goes out to enforce the law."

"I'll train 'im, Harry—jest give me 'bout a month to git it done," Elliott replied.

Joaquin watched Governor Brodie pin a five-point silver star badge on his shirtfront. The badge was inscribed "Arizona Rangers" with the number "11".

"Wear that badge proudly, son." Captain Rynning said.

"The man that wore that badge before you sure did. He died serving the citizens of the Arizona Territory."

Lieutenant Wheeler stepped forward and shook Joaquin's hand, congratulating him. He addressed the Governor. "Whatever happened with Ayala's pension, sir?"

"The legislature previously approved a pension for his widow—$25.00 a month for two years, this year the heartless bastards cut it in half."

"Well, I reckon it's somethin' fer Marie and the girls," returned Elliott. He swore his oath of allegiance, signed his sergeant's enlistment paper.

Governor Brodie concluded the meeting. "Thank you, gentlemen. Well done." He asked Elliott, "When do you plan to go after Chacon?"

"Well sir, I figger to get Joaquin trained up first. Thet'll give Tom and Harry time to work out things with them Mexicans one way or the other and get provisions together. Then we'll go get 'im, I reckon."

The Governor placed his arm around Elliott's shoulders. "Don't take offense, Elliott, but I don't want him draped over a saddle like the Indians you chased years ago." He slapped Elliott on the back affectionately. "I want him back here to stand trial ... then hung."

"Yessir. I heerd thet. I reckon I've changed some since them days."

With business concluded, Rynning, Wheeler, Elliott, and Joaquin walked out of the capitol, boarded the trolley, and headed back to the Adams Hotel. Joaquin's heart still pounded in his chest. *I'm a real Ranger.* He reached up and felt the silver star pinned to his shirt then looked down at it, pride swelling within him. Somehow, he would help capture the outlaw Indio Chacon. He knew he had a long way to go before he was up to the task ahead of him, but with Elliott's help he knew he would not fail. He had to make sure his family would be safe.

When he told Carmen he planned to join the Rangers and help hunt down his father's murderer, she stared at him for a long time. Then she said he should do whatever he thought was right.

Joaquin closed his eyes and relived their embrace, the smell of her hair—desert flowers after a thunderstorm—a natural sweet smell he would savor for a long, long time.

He promised her when he finished his year's enlistment with the Rangers, they would marry, if she was still willing.

Joaquin squared his shoulders. He would have to truly apply himself like he had never done before and come back alive to keep his promise.

CHAPTER FOURTEEN

Joaquin touched his spurs to his pony's flanks, and the little horse trotted up alongside Elliott's horse. Viento leisurely peered over at the four-legged competitor next to him. The horse's eyes seemed to twinkle; Joaquin thought maybe just a little bit like his master's did on occasion.

"Elliott, I didn't even know you had a ranch till my dad told me a few months back."

The old Ranger slowed his mount to a fast walk and looked over at the boy. "Don't reckon I ever had a need to advertise it to no one."

"What kind of a place is it?" Joaquin enjoyed walking his horse without the jarring trot gait.

Elliott tipped his old, battered gray Stetson back on his head, "It's 'bout all a man could want I reckon. It was jest the ticket fer me an' mah wife when we was first married." He paused. "Course it warn't nothin' like what she was used to bein's her pa owned one o' them big *ranchos* up in northern New Mexico Territory."

He smiled the natural lines and creases taking shape in his brown, leathery face. "She was the happiest gal I ever did know an' thet's a fact, *mi'ijo*."

They had been riding along the San Pedro River for several hours. Viento took the opportunity when he knew his master's mind was elsewhere, reaching down to grab large mouthfuls of grass. The horse munched contentedly on the lush riparian vegetation.

"Anyhow, it ain't a big spread as ranches in these here

parts go, but it's 'bout right fer me. I filed on the home-
stead, the hundred sixty acres, back in 1870 an' was able to
prove it up so it's all mine, free and clear. The rest o' the
land nearby is all federal an' mine fer the grazin' I reckon.
After I lost Maria and little Joaquin ... why, I thought o'
sellin' the whole shootin' match; lock, stock, an' barrel."

He reined his horse toward the river, "We'd best be wa-
terin' these hosses." Joaquin enjoyed the shade of the huge
cottonwood trees; he stepped down off his horse to drink
from the river, upstream from his horse. He used his hat to
pour water over his head and felt cooler for it.

The old Ranger was still talking, maybe more to himself
than his young companion. "Hao Li had to have a place to
live, I reckon. I owed him thet an' more."

"Who? What?" Joaquin, suddenly interested in what
the older man had to say.

"Hao Li. Ain't ya been payin' attention, *mi'jo?*"

"I guess I never heard anybody talking about ... well,
whatever you just said."

"Hao Li ... means great strength in Chinese. He's one
helluva man, thet's for shore."

"Huh ...?" Joaquin frowned.

"Have a seat here in the shade fer a spell, an' I'll tell
ya 'bout mah good friend. Hell, I jest call 'im Li fer short."
Joaquin sat down, leaning against a tree. "Ya see ... after
them Apaches killed ma wife an' baby boy, I went plumb
crazy—grievin' an' sech. I was in Bisbee an' hung out in
Brewery Gulch. I was drunk most o' the time, an' I kinda
took to the Orient Saloon 'an thet bad bunch what hung
out there. I even took some o' thet opium when I plumb
hit bottom on a drunken binge."

Elliott's eyes squinted, his tongue licked and pulled at
his full, white mustache. "Well anyhow, ole Li ... he found
me mostly dead out behind the saloon one night an' took me

to his place, a little shack in Bisbee. He showed me the right way o' thinkin' 'bout life an' some handy ways o' fightin'."

"This Li feller—where does he live?"

"On my ranch. Takes care of it fer me. Raises a few calves fer butcherin' 'an a helluva big garden ever' year."

The two of them rode on another hour, crossed the river to the east side, and Elliott pointed out his place nestled in among a large grove of cottonwood trees.

A small frame house painted white stood in the shade of the trees. The house had a front porch with a wooden rocking chair on the west end. The ranch house's roof was covered with wood shingles. A small barn stood solidly a short distance from the house with several corrals adjacent to it. A fenced pasture fully enclosed in barbed wire just north of the ranch buildings stuck out like a sore thumb to Joaquin; the pasture, a bright green, recently irrigated from the river appeared much more pleasant to him. His gaze continued to a smaller fenced-in piece of ground next to the house on the south side; a garden had been recently planted. Just beyond, but within reach of the house, stood a small unpainted privy. They rode up to the house, dismounted, and tied their horses to the hitchrack in front.

Elliott started up the steps of the porch and hollered out, "Li, *amigo*! Where are ya, *compadre*?"

A low, mellow voice answered from within the house, "Eh-we-ut? Is you, my fren?" Inside, an oriental man worked over a wood-burning cook stove. He looked up and smiled broadly. "You jest in time, Eh-we-ut. Suppa most ready." The man appeared to be maybe Elliott's age, and like Elliott, he had a litheness about him that seemed out of place.

"I kin see thet, Li, an' it smells mighty good." Elliott motioned toward Joaquin behind him. "This here's Joaquin, a new Ranger an' friend o' mine. He'll be stayin' with us fer a spell."

The Chinese man stopped his cooking activities, stepped toward Joaquin, and bowed. "How you do, mistah Hoe-kin?" He bowed politely again. "You ... most welcome mistah Hoe-kin. Excoose please." He then returned to his duties at the stove. Joaquin looked more closely at the man. He was neither tall nor short, but average in height, slender with definite oriental features. His hair was short and graying; he was clean-shaven and neat. The knees of his trousers were wet. *He's been working the garden.*

Joaquin liked the man immediately. "Li, it's a pleasure to know you, sir. Elliott speaks very highly of you."

"Mistah Eh-we-ut ... he very goot man ... goot to Li."

Elliott put an arm around the Chinese man's shoulders. "You ain't too shabby yourself, Li. Me an' Joaquin will put the hosses up. You shore ya got 'nough grub fer all of us to eat?"

Hao Li nodded. "Plenty food, Eh-we-ut."

As the two men walked their horses to the barn, Joaquin said, "I figger Li's a nice feller. I think I could learn to like him."

Elliott smiled, "Why, I shore hope so, *mijo*. You're goin' to be seein' a lot of 'im fer awhile—he'll be trainin' ya to fight." Once inside the barn, he dropped the reins on Viento and the horse stopped dead in his tracks. Elliott then stripped the saddle and saddle blanket from the horse and currycombed his lathered back.

Joaquin did the same for his paint horse. "Li ... he don't seem the fightin' kind. I mean—not just his size, but he's so nice 'an all," he mused.

"Thet's the whole idée, boy. Good fighters don't have to be big 'an mean. Why, I've whupped big 'uns jest like thet by beatin' 'em at their own game. Li showed me years ago thet ya fight better 'an tougher when ya ain't mad—ya let 'em use all thet hate 'an size against themselves."

Elliott reached up and unbuckled the throatlatch,

slipped the snaffle bit from Viento's mouth, and removed the bridle. The horse looked briefly at his master, as if thanking him for ending the long workday. Then the gray bay trotted easily on through the barn to the corral and water trough outside. Elliott tossed hay in the manger overlooking the corral.

Joaquin stood, watching Elliott. "I don't reckon I fully understand what you just said. It's hard for me to believe that nice man in there is a fighter."

Elliott tipped his head back and chuckled softly to himself. "When it comes to hand to hand fightin' ... no guns ... thet feller is the most dangerous man I've ever knowed. He don't know it yet, but he's goin' to be teachin' ya how to fight jest like he done fer me years ago."

Joaquin thought, *how in the ... just trust in Elliott.* He reached up, removed his horse's bridle, slapped him lightly on the rump; the paint eagerly joined Viento in the corral.

The old Ranger was talking. "Then I'm goin' to teach ya more'n ya ever want to know 'bout gun fightin'—arrestin' outlaws and low down bad men who break the law an' murder innocent folks like your dad." Elliott looked somberly at Joaquin. "When we're done, you'll be more ready fer the job than most; no garntees, but me 'an ole Li ...why, I reckon we'll do our best."

Elliott leaned back against the tack room door inside the barn and watched as Hao Li instructed Joaquin. "Mistah Hoe-kin, hit me. *Hit me.*" Joaquin just stood there. Elliott thought, *uh-oh, the boy's takin' a real likin' to the Chinaman.*

Elliott finally hollered, "Go on dammit! Knock his damn head off!"

"I can't ... *I can't hurt him.*"

"The hell ya say. I jest gave ya a *di*-rect order. *Hit him.*"

Joaquin's face darkened turning beet-red, his eyes flashed. He swung hard at the Chinese man with a right-handed haymaker punch. Li deftly dropped his head, stepped to his left slipping the blow, and as Joaquin swung around with his punch, he shoved Joaquin from behind, forcing him off-balance almost to the ground.

"Verie goot, Hoe-kin. You see how make ottha man beat self?" Li smiled. "Now, you try."

During the following week, the barn became Joaquin and Li's training ground. Elliott continued watching mostly. He could see the boy had strength, balance, and sincere interest in becoming a good fighter. But there was no fire—no win at all cost thinkin', the kind you had to have to survive in the violent world Elliott knew existed while enforcing the law. *He jest don't have the heart to hurt somebody bad—much less to kill a man if'n he had to.* And he was troubled by that.

He rubbed his chin, feeling the stubble, as Li showed Joaquin how to balance himself with his feet spread appropriately, his left leg forward and right leg back. His elbows in next to his ribs and belly, his hands open out in front of his face and, in particular, his chin.

Joaquin punched straight out at his adversary, hard with his first two knuckles to take the brunt of the blow, turning as he delivered the blow with all of his body weight behind him. Li slipped the punch. Off balance, Joaquin nearly fell to the ground. He laughed a short clipped laugh. As he recovered and turned to face Li, Elliott's voice, a metallic ring in it, stopped him in mid-stride.

"You think it's funny, boy ... when a man's whuppin' ya?"

Joaquin straightened his frame. His chest heaved, sweat ran down his face and neck. He dropped his arms to his side, his expression somber. "I just feel stupid ... and silly for messing up, *again.*"

"You'll get it right with practice. Ol' Li, he's damn good."

Elliott pursed his lips then toyed with his mustache. "What bothers me most is ya ain't got no—killer drive in ya. You're ... too damn nice ... an' afeered o' hurtin' a man."

Joaquin shouted, his eyes blazing, "I can kill that *son-of-a-bitch*, Chacon!" He turned to Li, his mouth set. "Let's get back at it."

A smile toyed at the old Ranger's mouth then disappeared. He watched in earnest as Li showed Joaquin how to move and use his adversary's strength and size to his advantage; how to slip and block punches. Then Li showed him the significance of using his feet and his legs for greater effect and power. Joaquin quickly found when he kicked with his legs and feet, he had far more power in his blows than with his arms and fists.

Li made him practice, practice, and practice. Joaquin balanced on his left foot and swung his right leg in a high, sweeping round-house kick at Li. The Chinese man slipped the kick with Joaquin falling heavily to the ground. He lay there, gasping for air.

"Elliott, I ... can't ... do it!"

"The hell ya say."

"It's too hard to learn." Joaquin swallowed hard, feeling the dry, cotton in his mouth. "I dunno ..."

"I ain't forcin' ya none. I never would've figgered *you* as a quitter, hoss."

Joaquin stood unsteadily. Li stepped toward him, smiled and said, "Mister Hoe-kin. You be goot fighter. I show now."

Elliott watched in fascination during the next several hours. The Chinaman slowly began to improve the boy's skills and attitude as a fighter. As an instructor, Li was damn good at fighting hand-to-hand, wiry and quick for his laid back, quiet personality. The man seemed ageless and possessed an inner calmness. All these years, Elliott had never seen him mad, or upset even when he was having a bad day—he jest accepted what he was given each day 'an made the most of it. Quiet, not mean but hard an' capable o' killin' when the need was there. *Hope it rubs off on the boy.*

Elliott was ever present as the training progressed, observing, but never again interfering or talking while the two other men were working in the barn. One evening after supper, Joaquin washed the supper dishes and stepped out on the porch to enjoy the cool night air. Elliott sat in the old rocking chair smoking a cigarette that he had just built.

"*¿Estas cansado, mi'jo?*

"*Si*. I'm all done in ... 'most ready for bed."

"Ya learnin' anythin'?"

Joaquin sat down on the porch, his face pensive. "Yessir. I just hope I can remember everything when I need to use it."

"I reckon it'll be second nature to ya, boy ... when the time comes."

"Where did the Chinese folks learn all this stuff anyhow?"

Elliott drew deeply on his cigarette, exhaling slowly. "The way I heerd it, a bunch of them Chinese monks got together years ago an' figgered jest how to take life—one day at a time. Then they figgered out how to fight like sumbitches. Right smart fellers ... them monks was."

He paused. "The whole idée is to *not* fight if'n ya kin help it, but if'n ya do—go whole hog. Like Li told ya, don't git mad an' lose your temper. Be the quiet one thet's always thinkin''an deadly when it comes down to it. *¿Comprende?*"

"Yessir, I think I do understand."

Elliott tossed his cigarette, stood up and started into the house, pausing at the door, "You ever been in a fight, boy?"

"I got in a fight once at school with the Watkins boy."

"Whup him ... did ya?"

"Pretty much a draw as I recall."

"You boys most likely shook hands when it was over. Right?"

"Well, we were friends after that …"

Elliott's voice had an edge in it. "The point I'm tryin' to make is—it ain't thet way in the real world—not when you're dealin' with no-good, *low*down bad men while *en*forcin' the law." Elliott peered into the darkness. "After ya fight—fists o' guns—there's no helping 'em up an' shakin' hands. Don't never give them bad men a leg up. You do an' they'll hurt ya bad, kill ya … or worse." He looked hard at Joaquin. "You gittin' my drift?"

"Yessir, I reckon so."

Bueno. We'll start trainin' with shootin' irons *manana.* Git yourself some sleep. I reckon you'll need it."

Morning came early for Joaquin. Rolling out of the bedroll to a sitting position on the floor, he looked grog-gily around the room. Dawn's faint light illuminated the horizon and the inside of the ranch house. Joaquin caught movement near the table. Elliott knelt in front of the cross that hung on the wall near the table, a rosary in his hands. Joaquin lay back on the bedroll and waited until Elliott made the sign of the cross and stood up.

After eating the breakfast Hao Li had prepared for all of them. Joaquin stepped out onto the porch, and breathed in the cool, fresh air. The cottonwood leaves rustled in the breeze, like a thick green blanket slowly twisting back and forth in the crisp spring air.

Elliott came out carrying a revolver, pistol belt and holster, skinning knife and sheath. He held them out to Joaquin. "These was your dad's—now they're yours."

Joaquin stared down at the worn .45 single action revolver encased in the old holster. Reaching out, he took the belt holster from Elliott almost dropping the heavy gun. *Dammit. Don't screw this up.* He buckled the belt and holster around his waist with difficulty. It was heavy, cumbersome and seemed to weigh him down. He felt uncomfortable with the gun belt on.

"You ever shoot a pistol?"

"No, never. I can shoot a rifle, though."

"I figgered as much. Ever' man carries his pistol different, but there's only one way thet's worked fer me ... on mah right side, belted up where the gun sets halfway between my wrist and elbow."

Elliott stepped off the porch, walked down by the river with Joaquin following closely behind. He squared off at a large cottonwood tree near the river. With Joaquin on his right side, he slowly demonstrated the draw. "As your hand comes up, grip the gun an' cock the hammer as you're drawin'. Bring your other hand over to help hold the gun out at eye level. Thet'll give ya a more steady shot. Thet pistol is mighty heavy to hold out one-handed fer a long spell an' still shoot well. Mostly, in a gunfight close-up ya won't need to use your weak hand, but if'n ya kin ... why, you'll shoot a whole lot better. Go on, try it."

Joaquin drew the revolver, forgetting to cock it as instructed. He almost lost his grip then reached out with his weak hand to hold the heavy pistol steady.

"Thet's the ticket, boy. But ya got to cock it—won't fire lessin' ya do."

Elliott then showed the boy how to properly load and unload the revolver. "In a gunfight ya kin shoot them bullets mighty quick—not even know when you're empty. Can't reload out in the open without gettin' shot. Maybe ya don't have time to reload. Thet's why I always carry me 'nother revolver, right here." He patted the leather shoulder holster tucked under his left armpit.

"When ya unload, load at the same time ... like this." Joaquin watched in fascination as Elliott drew the old revolver at his side. Magically, the old pistol appeared to be an extension of his very being. His knees were slightly bent as the right hand snaked up, cocking the pistol as it was drawn from the holster, and almost immediately fired as the gun left the holster. *Blam!*

Bark flew off the cottonwood tree where the heavy .45 slug hit dead center. Holding the revolver, strong hand supported by the weak, he quickly fired the remaining rounds into the same small area of the tree.

Joaquin shook his head. *My God, there's no way I'll ever shoot like that.*

Elliott opened the loading gate, extracted the spent cartridges and deftly loaded live rounds from his cartridge belt in five of the six chambers, leaving one unloaded. He turned the cylinder until the unloaded chamber was situated on top under the hammer.

He released the hammer and then spun the revolver on his right finger, twice forward then backward with the heavy pistol settling into place by its own weight in the well-oiled leather holster. "Always kick out an empty casing an' load a live round 'afore turning the cylinder to load more chambers. *"¿Comprende, mi'jo?"*

Joaquin digested what Elliott had just shown him. "I think so ... unload then reload each chamber of the cylinder so if you have to shoot before you've reloaded all six chambers, you'll at least be able to get a round or two off."

"I'd say you got the jest of it, boy. When you're through shootin' an' it's safe—load five chambers an' leave one open under the hammer so's ya don't blow your leg off when it's holstered. Jest be sure ya know which way the cylinder turns if'n ya shoot afore all them chambers is loaded."

Joaquin opened the cylinder of the revolver, fumbled with extracting the shells from the belt loops. He inserted shells into two chambers then dropped a shell. He shook his head, sighed and slowly loaded the other chambers, closing the cylinder.

"'Nother thing ... when ya draw, point an' shoot. Don't be worryin' 'bout lining up them sights. Use two hands to steady the gun. You ain't always got time to bring it up to eye level, 'pecially at close range. The idée is to draw fast an' shoot 'afore the bad guy does." The old Ranger's eyes twinkled. "Some like to hold the trigger back at close range an' fan the hammer fer fast firin'." He paused.

"Just point and it'll hit where I want to shoot?" asked Joaquin.

"You bet."

There's no way that's going to happen for me, thought Joaquin.

Elliott had Joaquin practice drawing, cocking, and pointing without firing the heavy revolver. Then he practiced cocking and shooting the old revolver. He missed the entire tree with the first three rounds. Finally, he was able to hit the tree by holding the revolver with both hands, taking his time with each shot.

At close range, Joaquin was amazed how accurately he placed his shots by pointing with the gun—like it was an extension of his finger. Eventually, Elliott had him shoot then move to cover or concealment—any tree, shrub, rock, but more importantly, to move and not stand in one location while shooting.

Just as Hao Li had required in the hand-to-hand fighting, Elliott made him practice, practice, and practice. Joaquin began to feel somewhat comfortable in handling and shooting the old .45 revolver that had belonged to his father. He wasn't fast like Elliott on his draw, but he could at least shoot the damn thing without blowing his own leg off.

As Joaquin retired for bed, he had difficulty in going to sleep. *I'm bone-weary ...how can I go on? I'm just not a very good shot with a pistol.* He thought about potential shootouts with seasoned outlaws. *Hell, they can just wait me out ... maybe smoke a cigarette ... then allow me to shoot myself while I'm fumbling around trying to shoot them.* He almost laughed at the thought. *What'll I do if I have to face a real gunman? Run? Did I make the right decision in becoming a Ranger?* His mind continued to churn over drawing, pointing, shooting, sight picture and alignment. *And don't forget to cock the damn thing when you draw ...don't mess that up again.*

After a full week of handgun training, Joaquin became comfortable in wearing the pistol belt with the heavy revolver. He moved the holster from the cross draw position on the pistol belt to the right side. As directed by Elliott, he cleaned the old revolver religiously every night. Elliott warned him that he could not afford to have a malfunction when using the handgun, and that it was essential to properly clean the weapon thoroughly after firing it, no exceptions. *Your life an' your feller officers depend on you bein' ready at all times to use deadly force, if'n necessary.* The old Ranger's words rang out to him, bouncing aimlessly back and forth inside his head. He decided he had a bad headache, took a deep breath, rolled over and finally went to sleep.

Standing alongside Elliott, Joaquin studied his targets from the day before. *Lord have* mercy, *I sure did awful yesterday.* He sighed. "Am I ever goin' to be as good as you?"

"You'll do fine, *mi'jo.*" Elliott grinned. "You're jerkin' the trigger—slow an' steady as she goes." He set up multiple targets, which were papers, nailed to three trees. "Draw an' shoot two rounds at each target."

Joaquin moved quickly, drawing, shooting at each target, and the last two rounds at the final target from the kneeling position. He quickly reloaded and pointed his revolver covering the targets.

"Damn fine job o' shootin', *mijo*." Elliott beamed while looking at the tight group of hits. "Why, you're a real *pistolero* ... I kin shore 'nough see thet—a better shot with thet handgun than your daddy ever was."

Elliott motioned for them to sit under the shade of an old cottonwood tree along the San Pedro River. The afternoon breeze rustled the canopy of the huge magnificent trees, most likely sheltering many others on numerous occasions in by-gone years. Joaquin saw him wince as he lowered himself to the ground. He quickly repositioned his right knee.

Joaquin cleared his throat. "Can I ask you ... a personal question?"

"I reckon so."

"Do you believe in God, Elliott?"

The old Ranger re-positioned his knee yet again. "Yep."

"Why?" queried Joaquin.

"Well, there was a time when I never believed in much of anything. The only thing I thought of ... hoped fer ... was dyin'. I reckon I hated ever' thing an' ever' one, includin' Gawd."

The warm sunshine found its way somehow through the foliage, warming them; the clear, blue sky incessant, accentuating the green riparian area where they were seated. Elliott licked his lips. "The bottom line is thet bein' outdoors all mah life ... why, I jest know there's shore 'nough a Gawd what made it all."

Joaquin continued. "What if you're wrong, and there ain't a God?"

Elliott sighed deeply, leaned back against the tree, and took his hat off running his fingers through his thick white hair. He gazed at the young man sitting next to him. "I reckon you'll have to figger out the answer to thet all by your lonesome, *mi'jo*. One thing I do know ... I'd rather be one o' them fellers thet has believed in Gawd an' is plumb ready to go 'afore Him when I die." He paused chewing at his lower lip. "If'n there ain't no Gawd, why I reckon it won't matter no ways."

Elliott replaced his hat and leaned forward. "I got some lawman things to talk to ya 'bout. First thing, always watch a man's hands. If'n he figgers on hurtin' or killin' ya, it'll be with his hands. If'n ya can't see 'em when you're arrestin' a man, *¡Cuidado!* Them hairs on the back of your neck had best be standin' up. He kin kick hell outta ya if'n ya ain't watchin', but with his hands—he kin use a gun, a knife, a club an' kill ya dead."

Second thing; get the drop on them bad men. Walk on past then draw your gun an' throw down on 'em. Make 'em raise them hands high.

"Yessir." Joaquin picked up a flat rock, threw it out along the water's surface. It skimmed for a ways, slowed and disappeared beneath the surface.

"'An 'nother thing ... when ya got 'em covered with their hands up, you tell 'em one at a time to unbuckle them gun belts with the left hand an' drop 'em to the ground. Then make 'em step way back with them hands high whilst' ya pick the gun belts up."

Elliott pulled a blade of grass, chewed on it awhile. "Most folks is right handed ... you remember thet. Use your hoss or anything else fer cover when you're dealing with bad men—anything to keep 'em from thinkin' they got a clean easy shot at ya."

Elliott stood up and started for the barn. He turned toward the boy still seated beneath the tree. "We're burnin' daylight, git your paint hoss saddled up. We'll do some shootin' from horseback."

Elliott and Joaquin rode several miles out from the

ranch. Elliott had Joaquin shoot at targets with his six-shooter while galloping. He emphasized that the handgun was best for accuracy from horseback. Then he had Joaquin practice shooting with the rifle.

Elliott called out a target such as a tree or tree stump and had Joaquin slip off his horse's rump while simultaneously removing his rifle from the scabbard. Joaquin dropped to the ground and shot at the target. Elliott shouted out where each round was hitting.

Finally, Joaquin was allowed to use the adjustable sights on his 1895 Winchester. He practiced hard at becoming a good rifle shot and day by day he got better. Another week passed with long days of training.

As the men rode into the barn and dismounted, the evening sky was afire with a bright orange glow in the west. The cumulus clouds accentuated the fading sun as it began its slow descent below the horizon.

Elliott eased his weight onto his good leg as he threw the stirrup over his saddle and began to remove the latigo from the cinch ring. "Ya reckon you're 'bout trained out, *mi'jo?*"

Joaquin chuckled as he unsaddled the paint. "Like you say, Elliott, I'm plumb wore down to the nub."

He deposited his saddle and blanket on the saddletree in the tack room. He walked back out and brushed his horse down. The paint horse trotted on out through the barn into the corral.

Joaquin turned. "Elliott, you ever been afraid of ... dying?"

The old ranger stopped in mid-stride then continued on into the tack room. He returned to brush Viento without replying. He stopped what he was doing, tipped his hat back on his head. "Ever' one dies, boy ... one time or 'nother. Ain't nothin' to be afraid of. Hell, dyin's the easy part. It's the livin' thet sometimes scares the hell outta ya." He finished brushing the horse's back, unbuckled the throatlatch and removed the bridle. As Viento hurried out to the water trough, Elliott turned to Joaquin, who was waiting patiently.

"When ya git in a fight with gunplay an' the lead starts flyin', you'll know *real* fear, *mi'jo*. Most likely you'll be so scared you'll want to freeze up ... wet your pants ... maybe run. Don't let thet git to ya. Know thet all of us gits scared. It's natural in them sit-i-a-tions. Ya jest gotta push the fear aside—go on ahead an' git the job done proper-like."

Elliott put his arm around Joaquin's shoulder. "I reckon you'll do fine. Ya sure got the makin's of a real man an' you're one trained up feller. I was goin' to tell ya thet we're about set fer headin' down to Mexico. It's 'bout time we paid Chacon a visit."

"When do we leave?" Joaquin nearly shouted.

"In the mornin'. I reckon we'll swing by your folks' place, help out with the spring roundup fer a few days. You kin see your family an' thet 'lil Carmen gal then we'll head on down to Douglas."

"I'll say goodbye to Li tonight. I've sure grown to like him."

"He shore thinks the world of you too, Joaquin."

Together, they walked back to the house. The light in the southwestern sky dimmed slowly into total darkness, akin to a kerosene lantern slowly being extinguished. Joaquin thought about what lay ahead for him during the next year. Was he up to the task? Would he perform when it was his time to do so? Only time would tell. One thing he was sure of—he wouldn't let Elliott or Li down. He took a deep breath and stepped into the ranch house.

CHAPTER FIFTEEN

"Let's go to the ol' pueblo! What do ya say, *mi'jo?*" Elliott had just finished talking to a Ranger outside the ranch house. It was early morning. A mourning dove spoke from atop the house, another from the tree canopy near the San Pedro River.

Joaquin stepped out on the porch. He ran his fingers through his thick brown disheveled hair. "I thought we were goin' to the ranch then to Douglas and Mexico after Chacon?" He didn't want to hear a change in plans.

"We will ... we will, boy. The Cap'n sent a rider fer me, tellin' me to go to Tucson—palaver with the *U*nited States Attorney 'bout Chacon 'afore we go on down an' git 'im." He grinned as he stepped up on the porch beside Joaquin. "Ole JLB, by Gawd, Alexander."

"Who?" asked Joaquin.

"J.L.B. Alexander, the *U*nited States Attorney."

Joaquin frowned, disappointed in any delay to go after Chacon. "So you said, but who is he?"

"He's the man who'll prosecute thet son-of-a-bitch Chacon when we catch him. That's who he is—an' he's a feller Rough Rider. Fought with us in Cuba, he did." Elliott shook his head, smiled again. He looked at Joaquin. "Hell, I ain't been to the ol' pueblo fer a long while. Let's go—today, *mi'jo.*"

Joaquin put his hands in his pockets, stared at his dusty boots. "I dunno ... I don't reckon you need me taggin' along."

"The hell I don't. You're comin'—won't take no fer an answer. Besides its *o*fficial business I'm talkin' 'bout." He held Joaquin by his shoulders. "Git thet shiny badge and gun belt on, an' your party'n clothes, we're goin' to town." Elliott laughed, a giddy laugh, and stepped off the porch. "Thet's an order, by Gawd."

As they rode through the little settlement of Benson located along the banks of the San Pedro River, the day was warming; Joaquin watched in fascination as the desert heat waves shimmered, undulated, disappeared then re-appeared again. The Rangers varied the horses' gaits; walking, trotting, loping, as they rode toward Tucson, nestled beneath the Rincon Mountains. Several hours passed and he was finally able to see past Rincon Peak, the tall rocky sentinel of the Rincons. Mica Mountain stood prominently to the north in the late morning sunshine.

It was late afternoon when the tired, dusty Arizona Rangers rode into the old pueblo. Joaquin's paint horse walked impatiently alongside Viento. Mud huts made of adobe lined the streets. Joaquin saw Elliott make the sign of the cross; he looked up and noticed the tall belfry of the mission church ahead of them in the distance. They traveled down Congress Street then to Fourth Avenue, stopping in front of an adobe structure. They stepped down and tied their horses to the hitch rack. A rough sign out in front was titled "*Mamacita's-La Comida Buena.*"

Joaquin followed Elliott into the darkened interior. As his eyes adjusted to the change from bright sunshine, he scanned the room full of tables and people eating, talking. Elliott walked directly to a table situated in the corner of the room, Joaquin followed. A handsome middle-aged man stood as Elliott approached. He wore a new-looking suit and appeared very official to the young Ranger.

The man smiled broadly at Elliott, extended his hand. "You ol' codger. How the hell have you been?" They shook hands, laughed, and slapped each other on the back.

"I'm fine, JLB. Jest fit as a fiddle, I reckon. You?"

"Good, Elliott." He gazed at the old Ranger. "You've not changed one bit, *amigo*." He turned to Joaquin. "And this is ...?"

"This here's our new re-cruit, Joaquin Campbell. He's Lou's boy." He pointed at the suited man. "*Mijo*, meet Captain Joseph L.B. Alexander of Troop C, Rough Riders ... an' appointed United States Attorney by Teddy Roosevelt hisself."

"Pleased to meet you, son. I remember your dad in Cuba." Alexander laughed, an easy laugh, motioned to the table. "Let's get something to eat—my treat."

The hungry men ate supper then got down to business. Alexander spoke softly to Elliott. "I've got statements from two witnesses who saw Chacon gun down Bob Williams. They're both Mexicans who were present on the ranch the day of the murders. No one seems to have witnessed the killing of the ranch hand; however, we've got Chacon committing a felony, first-degree murder at best."

Elliott leaned forward. "What 'bout them jurors? Will they believe *Mexicanos*—JLB, you know how some o' them folks is."

Alexander shook his head. "I know ... I know, but almost everyone in the territory wants Chacon to swing for what he's done over the years. I don't think it will be a problem." He straightened in his chair. "I understand from Tom Rynning one of the outlaws told you that Chacon murdered Williams."

"Uh huh ... jest 'afore he died."

"I'll need a written statement from you—you'll have to testify in court. Maybe the Judge will allow the hearsay evidence since the man's dead." Elliott nodded. Alexander turned to Joaquin. "Also, I plan to prosecute Chacon for your father's murder and felony assault on the ranch hand,

Domingo Ponce. Ponce has already given me his statement."

"Thank you, sir," Joaquin said. *You better convict the son-of-a-bitch.*

"Sounds like you got things purty well sewed up, JLB," retorted Elliott.

"I sure hope so." Alexander interlaced his fingers; the forefingers toyed with his lips. "Elliott, you've got to bring the son-of-a-bitch back to the States for trial. Don't kill 'im, you hear?"

"I reckon it'll be up to him ... but me an' Joaquin, we'll do our best."

"All right, *amigo*, it's all I ask." He paused. "I need this trial—and to win a conviction."

"Them politics again, eh," asked Elliott.

"I'm afraid so." The man's face clouded in thought.

Elliott stood up, stretched his right knee. "We shore appre-shate them vittles, JLB. Now I need me a good drink o' liquor down the street at the *sa*-loon—wash thet trail dust down an' warm mah innards 'afore mah bedtime." Joaquin stood.

"Yes, my sentiments exactly. Don't forget to get that statement to me before you leave in the morning." Alexander stood and shook hands with the Rangers. "Good luck, gentlemen." He looked at both of them. "Do your job and bring him in—I'll do mine—and he'll hang."

Their spurs raked the board sidewalk as they made their way down the street toward the saloon. The sun had set and dusk descended once again on the old pueblo. Joaquin thought, *I wonder how Elliott does it. I'm bone-weary, and he don't even look tired.* When they had almost reached the saloon, the batwing doors swung out suddenly, a man ran out, directly into Elliott bumping him into Joaquin.

Wide-eyed, he yelled, "Don't you go in there! Men holdin'" up the saloon ... *guns*." He gasped, stumbled off the sidewalk into the dusty street. The man looked visibly shaken.

"Easy now, hoss. What the *hell* are ya sayin'?"

The man swallowed hard, placed his hands on his knees to catch a deep breath. He looked up at Elliott. "I'm tellin' you to run, you damn fool! Bad men—kilt bartender— stealin' money." He licked his lips. "I'm goin' ... to find ..." Then he saw the silver stars on both men's shirts. "Wait a minute—you *are* the law!"

Elliott dismissed the man, his eyes hard. "Yessir ... thet's what we're here for." He spoke to Joaquin without turning as he moved toward the door, "When we go through the door—do it quick an' step to my left away from me." With that he was gone, inside the saloon.

Joaquin's heartbeat quickened. He licked dry lips, drew his six-shooter and bolted through the door, moving to his left as instructed. The interior was dim with little ambient light and it was early for all the lamps to be aglow. He made out Elliott striding toward the bar, and beyond him two men, one wearing overalls. *Overalls? What the hell ... some sodbuster robbin' the place?* He saw the man turn, the eyes ablaze, and a large revolver in his fist.

Joaquin watched in horror as Elliott strode forward, not hesitating or drawing his revolver. His own revolver came up without him thinking about bringing it to bear on the target. *Shoot 'im! Shoot 'im! I can't—can't pull—the trigger.* Swallowing hard, he remembered to cock the single-action .45 then pressed forward toward the men at the bar. His finger tightened on the trigger.

"Rangers—drop your guns an' throw them hands up!" roared Elliott.

Overalls' revolver belched flame, bucked in his hand. Elliott, close now, stood solid. *Thank God! He's not hit.*

Joaquin did not see Elliott's draw, but he heard the thunderous explosions of Elliott's six-shooter. Two quick shots evenly spaced. Overalls flew backward, the left side of his head blown off. The second man, who also was armed, stood, tittering on his feet, the handgun slipped out of his hand, clattering to the floor. Grimacing with pain, he looked down incredulously at the red crimson blossoming on his shirtfront.

Elliott stepped forward and shoved the man roughly to the floor. He reached down, picked up the handgun, and turned to Joaquin. His blue eyes softened. "Git thet overall feller's gun, *mi'jo.*"

Joaquin shook uncontrollably as he holstered his revolver. He picked up the outlaw's gun. *I'm so sorry, Elliott. Dammit! I couldn't shoot ...what's the matter with me?* He looked once more at the dead man. Blood flowed freely onto the dirty saloon floor from the man's head—what there was left of it, anyways. Joaquin stumbled to a darkened corner of the saloon. He heard Elliott talking to someone, feet rushing into the saloon, the batwings swishing back and forth. He knelt down and threw up the free Mexican supper, courtesy of ole JLB, by Gawd, Alexander. He gagged tasting bile in his throat. Crying silently in the darkness, tears trickled down his cheeks. *I won't give up, Dad ...I won't quit!*

CHAPTER SIXTEEN

J oaquin stepped into the Ranger Headquarters—a two-room adobe building located on the south end of Fifteenth Street in Douglas, Arizona—clutching his canvas bedroll under his arm. Elliott was talking to a rotund man wearing glasses, sitting behind a desk.

Elliott turned to Joaquin. "This here's Sergeant Arthur Hopkins." As the two men shook hands, Elliott continued, "He's Captain Rynning's right hand man. He does a helluva job runnin' the office fer us Rangers."

Sergeant Hopkins smiled at the young recruit. "Welcome to the Arizona Rangers, Joaquin. We're proud to have you come aboard." He gestured. "You can stash your gear in the next room."

Elliott and Joaquin walked together into the adjoining room, cluttered with bedrolls, personal gear, saddles, tack, and guns. Three men awaited them. A tall, stocky, dark-complected man extended his hand to Joaquin. He wore a black, wide-brimmed sombrero covered with dust. As he smiled, his even, white teeth showed clearly beneath his dark handlebar mustache that was twisted tightly and curved upward on each end. A fancy pearl handled six-shooter in a glossy black holster was tied down on his right leg. His pant legs were tucked into his high-topped black leather boots.

"Howdy, Joaquin. Mah name's Wade ... Bill Wade. Wade turned to Elliott. "Now thet Harry's promoted, ah reckon you're the sergeant, eh?"

Elliott moved past Wade toward an empty bunk bed. "I reckon so, Bill." He tossed his bedroll down, and walked back to Wade, taking his time. *Uh-oh, some bad blood between the two of 'em,* thought Joaquin. Elliott looked directly into the man's eyes, then over at the other two men, who were seated at the table. He asked softly, "You fellers okay with thet?"

Wade was quick to answer. "Helluva pick, Elliott. Why, I can't think of anyone better-suited fer the job ... 'cepting maybe me." He laughed. "Thet is someday when you're too damn old to do the job anymore."

Elliott's eyes twinkled and a semblance of a smile formed on his deeply tanned face. "When thet day comes ... you'll be the first feller thet I tell, Bill." He turned to Joaquin, gestured toward the two men seated at the table. "This here is Frank Shaw an' Chapo Carter. Chapo started with the Rangers in '01 alongside me. Frank's been with us more'n a year now."

Shaw stood and shook hands with Joaquin. He was of medium height, slender, appeared easy-going and good-natured. He was clean-shaven, having recently had his dark curly hair cut short. His handsome tanned face broke into a grin. "Glad to meet you, Joaquin. If you ever need anything from another young pup, why, just holler at me—I'll tell you I have absolutely no idea—then I'll holler for Elliott, Bill, or Chapo." Joaquin joined in his laughter as the two shook hands.

Joaquin turned to Carter, who had been cleaning a Spanish-Mauser rifle on the table. He appeared middle-aged and in good health, shorter than Joaquin with short curly reddish hair tinted gray near his temples. His bowlegs and brown leathery face indicated many years horseback under the incessant southwestern sun.

"Proud to meet ya, son. Any friend of Elliott's is a friend

of mine." He smiled and nodded. "Fer thet matter, any son of Lou Campbell's is shore 'nough a friend. I fought in Cuba with your dad and ole Elliott there."

A shrill ringing noise came from the office. Joaquin jumped.

Bill Wade guffawed. "What's the matter, boy? Ain't ya never heerd a telephone 'afore?"

"No sir. I ain't seen one before neither. I've seen telegraphs though and watched 'em work."

Wade's eyes squinted. "At your age? I'll bet ya ain't seen or done a whole lot of things in life ... that be 'bout right?"

"I reckon not, Bill. I've mostly lived on my folk's ranch for the most part," replied Joaquin.

"Well, no matter, boy. I'll make sure you get a proper ed-i-ca-tion."

Sergeant Hopkins shouted from the office, "Sergeant Elliott. I've got Captain Rynning on the phone. He wants to talk to you."

Elliott strode into the office and Joaquin heard him talking for several minutes. *Talkin' into a telephone! Wait till Carmen hears about this. Now all he needed was to see one of them horseless carriages that he'd heard about.* When Elliott completed the conversation, he returned to the living quarters, Sergeant Hopkins trailing behind him. "Thet was Tom. There's trouble up in Morenci with strikin' miners. He said the eight-hour a day workweek was passed by the territorial legislature, 'an them minin' companies has tried to cut the miner's wages from $2.50 to $2.00 a day." Elliott scratched the back of his neck. "'Bout 3,000 miners has walked off the job figgering they can't make it like when they was working ten hours a day. Anyhow, to make things worse, Whites got the raise but the Mexicans, Italians, and Slovakians was told they wasn't gettin' no raise."

Wade snarled, "Damned greasers, dagoes, and bohunks

don't de-serve what Whites got coming!"

Joaquin frowned.

Elliott looked sharply at Wade and held up his hand. "Hold it, Bill. Let me finish. Tom says they got some sorta labor feller stirring 'em up and passing out free liquor. The Governor's worried thet some folks might git hurt or they might de-stroy mine property." He let that sink in. "He's ordered us—all twenty-four Rangers up there to re-store order."

"What about the sheriff? Why the hell ain't he taking care of it?" retorted Carter.

"Sheriff Parks from Solomonville is up there with 'bout sixty deputies thet he jest swore in; you know, store clerks 'an sech. They ain't been doin' too well so far. The National Guard and Army may be sent, but fer now, they want us to leave first thing in the mornin' on the train fer Morenci an' handle things till the military gits there."

Chapo Carter sat down at the table, and spoke with an edged voice, "I don't reckon I signed on with the Rangers to be herdin' a bunch o' miners around—I don't like it 'atall."

"I don't reckon I do neither, Chapo, but orders is orders. It ain't up to us to question 'em. I reckon we'll go 'an git the job done ... like it or not."

That's showin' 'em some, Elliott, thought Joaquin.

Bill Wade laughed loudly and snorted. "Well, I don't mind teachin' them bastards a thing or two. Who the hell do they think they are anyway? *The sons-of-bitches.*"

"Thet's enough, Bill," Elliott said. "All of us will go as ordered an' I don't want to hear no more about it." He turned to Hopkins standing to one side. "That includes you, Arthur ... Captain's orders. "An' he wants you to git word to all the others thet ain't here."

"That's fine by me, Elliott. Who will man the station?"

"The new recruit. What's his name?"

"Kidder. Jeff Kidder," replied Hopkins.

"Yeah. Kidder's not had trainin' yet, 'an the Captain wants him to stay here. Whatever all of you need done, git it done today. Be ready to board the train early in the mornin'." Elliott turned to Joaquin. "Chacon an' Mexico will have to wait, *mi'jo.*"

Joaquin tried not to show his disappointment. What the heck, he was hired on for a year anyways.

That night he did not sleep well, thinking about Carmen. How he wished he were with her. She was his best good friend, always there for him and doggone it, without a doubt, the best looking girl in the territory. He remembered their last conversation just before coming to Douglas.

He and Elliott had helped with the spring roundup since his dad was not there anymore. His mother, Domingo, and Carmen all looked tired and worn down. His mother's hair was almost all gray now, and although she worked hard at appearing to be happy, he knew that was not so. Domingo still had a large scar on the left side of his head where the large caliber bullet from a rustler's gun had burned its searing path.

He and Carmen sat out on the porch that evening, holding hands and talking. She told him that maybe they shouldn't get married—marrying her could cause problems for him in the community. There were many who did not condone an Anglo marrying a Mexican. She asked, "What about our children? Will they be allowed to attend the school for Whites or be outcasts for Whites and Mexicans alike?" She was afraid for their future and his welfare while working in law enforcement.

Honestly, he had no answers for her. He worried about the future, too. He told her he loved her with all his heart. And together, they would deal with any problems that arose—their families would be there for them and in the end, it was all that mattered in life. Then he kissed her forehead and held her tight, feeling her soft warmth next to him. She smiled, her sad, brown eyes realizing more of her fears.

He knew then just as he had always known, she was his girl, his best good friend, and no one ... nothing would ever keep her from him. He'd see to that.

CHAPTER SEVENTEEN

The northbound train arrived in Morenci Sunday evening and the Rangers went to work immediately. They carried their rifles and prominently displayed their badges on their shirtfronts and vests. Captain Rynning and Sheriff Parks set up a command center at a local hotel in Morenci.

Elliott watched quietly as bands of striking miners roved the darkened streets. Chapo Carter walked over to where he was standing.

"Don't look to be a good de-tail fer us."

"I reckon not." Elliott cradled the .30-.40 Winchester in his left arm.

"There's so damn many o' 'em."

"I reckon so."

Carter frowned, placing the butt of the Spanish-Mauser against his gun belt. "You ain't fer talkin' much, are ya?"

"I reckon not, Chapo." A smile toyed at the corner of his mouth.

Large crowds of men traveled back and forth between Morenci and a large lime pit quarried out of a hilltop overlooking Morenci. Barrels of whiskey were available there, and the strike had become festive with the miners becoming bolder. There was talk of damaging mine property, looting company stores, and killing gringos.

A Chicago agitator by the name of W.H. Lastaunau had been dispatched to the Clifton-Morenci-Metcalf mining district. Lastaunau was nicknamed "Mocho" or crippled hand by the Mexicans. Mocho had expertly organized the

miners to strike against the mine operators. The Rangers'
squads patrolled, scouting the town. Tension was mounting,
but there was no trouble that night.

Elliott and his squad arrived back at the hotel lobby. It
was late; Elliott's stomach growled. He was hungry, but he
had business to attend to first. Elliott stopped mid-lobby,
his squad in tow.

"You boys git somethin' to eat. I'll be along." He watched
Wade, Hopkins, Carter, Shaw, and Joaquin shuffle over to a
table in the restaurant. Rynning and Wheeler were seated
at another table smoking cigarettes.

"Howdy, Elliott. Pull up a chair, amigo," Harry Wheeler
said.

Elliott cradled his rifle in his left arm as he stepped
up to the table. "Thanks Harry." He nodded to Captain
Rynning. "Howdy, Tom."

"I'll bet it's been a long day, Elliott. Will you sit with
us—have something to eat?" Rynning motioned to a chair.

Elliott shuffled his feet, his spurs jingling against the
board floor.

"Naw, I reckon I'll eat with mah boys. But thanks jest
the same."

"Suit yourself. Did you find out anything worthwhile?"

"Well ... what with all the tension an' booze flowin' like
it is, this place is 'bout ready to explode. But I reckon you
an' Harry already know thet. I'd say most of the troublemak-
ers is coming from thet old lime pit north of town. Thet's
where they're taking all the whiskey. I didn't go up there
with mah men. I figgered we'd draw too much attention."
Elliott shifted the rifle. "After I eat, I figger on easin' up
there myself to take a look see."

"What do you think about tomorrow ... where to deploy?"
Wheeler asked.

Elliott sighed, mulling options over in his head. "The

badun's will be comin' from the lime pit. Most likely they'll sleep it off tonight an' they'll start all over agin tomorrow with the drinkin' and meetings. By late mornin', early afternoon at the latest, they'll be whipped into a frenzy an' talked into comin' down the hill if'n they want to cause trouble."

Wheeler nodded his head. "That's what we figured. It seems to be where most of the activity with the strike leaders is taking place. Mocho is supposed to be there, and he's stirring up a lot of the hate and discontent."

"Did them other Rangers make it in?" asked Elliott.

"All of them finally made it in," answered Rynning. "I want you and your men to eat, rest up tonight, then deploy a skirmish line by mid-morning just above the Chase Creek crossing on the road that goes up to the lime pit. I've made arrangements for rooms for all of you here at the hotel."

"When they do come down from thet pit ..." Elliott paused. "Well, there'll be a passel of 'em, maybe hundreds— maybe more. You reckon jest the six of us kin stop 'em?"

"You'll have to. I'll send Harry over in the morning to help you out. It's the best I can do. Sheriff Parks' deputies stationed up at the Longfellow Mine northeast of town have been overrun and disarmed. I've got to take some men up there and get control of the place."

Rynning was obviously frustrated. "Then we have to protect the Detroit Copper Company mill and store. Hell, I've got intelligence that these miners have cached weapons all over town and even up in the hills. I'll have the rest of the Rangers take all that on. I'm sorry, but Harry is all I can give you for tomorrow."

"I reckon we'll make do, Tom." Elliott replied. "We'll see ya in the mornin' then, Harry." The sharp pain in his knee made him wince as he stood. Walking away from the table, he tried not to limp.

After supper, Elliott removed his badge and pistol belt

then walked the quarter mile up to the lime pit from Chase Creek. Pulling his hat down low over his face, he sauntered into the festivities inside the pit. Free whiskey flowed from barrels; many of the miners were drunk, and all of them irate with the mining companies for not raising their hourly wages. Several men stood up and gave speeches, further inciting the men. One man in particular seemed to be everywhere, shouting encouragement to the other strike leaders and the miners who would listen to him. *Must be thet fiery Austrian—Lastaunau, they was talkin' 'bout.*

Elliott melded into the crowd and spoke only Spanish when it was absolutely necessary to speak. He hung around for an hour or so getting a feel for the miners, the strike leaders and what he might have to deal with the next day.

When he was ready to leave the lime pit, he noticed Lastaunau walking alone ahead of him and headed down the road toward Morenci. Elliott could not believe his good luck. *Hell, even a blind hog gits an acorn now an' agin.* He slowly eased unnoticed out of the pit and down the darkened road. *It's shore dark out...blacker'n inside o' damn cow out here.* Moments later he was able to make out the short stocky man walking ahead of him.

As the man turned quickly toward the sound of someone approaching him, Elliott asked, *"¿Quien es?"* He moved quickly up alongside the shorter man. Lastaunau continued walking down the road.

Elliott pulled his pistol from his shoulder holster and stuck it in the man's ribs. His icy voice cut the night air, "Arizona Ranger, Lastaunau. You're under arrest. Keep your mouth shut an' keep movin'." The startled man tried to stop in the road, but Elliott grabbed his arm and forcefully pushed him down the road toward Morenci.

"I ... am ... Lastaunau," he stammered. "You have no right to do this ..."

"The hell I don't. I have a warrant fer your arrest. You best keep walkin' an' be quiet; jest pray I don't gut shoot ya afore we git to town."

Lastaunau kept his mouth shut and both men made it safely to the hotel where Elliott turned the strike leader over to Sheriff Jim Parks. Rynning and Wheeler were pleased. Elliott couldn't believe his good luck in making the arrest. He just hoped that it would help them avoid bloodshed the following day.

The next morning Elliott and his men walked out to the north end of Morenci to Chase Creek and the old road leading up to the lime pit. By mid-morning swirling dark clouds controlled the sky laying a heavy coldness in the air. The Rangers wore jackets and had their rain slickers with them. Their pockets were filled with extra rifle and handgun ammunition. Pursuant to orders from their captain, the six men formed a skirmish line on the south side of the creek, using available rocks and trees for cover on either side of the road.

It began to drizzle, and the morning air cooled considerably. Elliott pulled his jacket collar up around his neck and his hat down onto his head as he peered north toward the lime pit. His rifle was cradled in his left arm. At the sound of someone approaching, he looked back toward town. Lieutenant Harry Wheeler walked down the road toward him, wearing his rain slicker and carrying a shotgun.

Joaquin hunkered down behind a boulder on the south side of Chase Creek. A surprise downpour thoroughly soaked him before he donned his rain slicker. When the wind picked up, his body chilled and he shook uncontrollably. *Why am I trembling so badly—nervous or just plain cold?*

Elliott had placed him adjacent to the road on the left side with Carter and Shaw. Elliott and Wheeler stood in the road with Wade and Hopkins on the right side. The men on either side of the road were behind cover—boulders, trees, dead fall, anything to give them an advantage if a fight occurred.

Joaquin heard yelling and the unmistakable sound of feet trampling in their direction. The rain had let up, but the presence of dark threatening skies presented an ominous backdrop to a group of men, possibly hundreds of miners, coming toward them. Once they saw the two Rangers in the road, they began yelling and waving their arms with fists clenched. Some of the men were armed with picks, shovels, and clubs. Others carried firearms.

Joaquin's throat was dry, and he fervently wished he had urinated earlier when he had the chance. Elliott and Wheeler shifted their long guns to point at the oncoming mass of men.

Elliott calmly called out to his men, "You boys pick out them thet's got guns an' draw a bead on 'em. If they try to shoot, you take 'em out. Harry an' I will take care o' the leaders an' them out in front."

The men slowed as they approached the Rangers in the road on the opposite side of the creek. Then they saw the other officers behind cover with weapons pointed at them.

One of the miners stepped forward. "My name's Salcido. I represent these men." He gestured toward those behind him. "You men are impeding our right-of-way. Move aside! Move aside, I said ... or we'll run you over."

Wheeler cocked both barrels of his shotgun. "Arizona Rangers. I'm issuing you a lawful order to stop, turn around, and head back up the hill to the pit. Now!"

Salcido attempted to stop; apparently realizing the Rangers confronting him meant business. However, the huge mass of men surging from behind, unaware of what was going on at the front, shoved him forward.

Joaquin raised his own Winchester .30-.40 rifle and covered one of the miners carrying a rifle. He heard Salcido shout, "We want Lastaunau. We know that he's being kept at the hotel in town, and we mean to get him."

"You'll get no one. Now you men clear outta here. That's an order!" retorted Wheeler.

One of the men in front armed with a pick, raised it and charged Wheeler shouting, "*¡Maten todos los gringos!*"

The double barrel shotgun bucked in Wheeler's hands as he fired from the hip. The man was jerked erect and flopped to the ground like a pole-axed bull.

Joaquin saw the men hesitate, almost as if everyone and everything was suspended in time, but only for that split-second. Then all hell broke loose. The man he had been covering raised his rifle. Without hesitation, Joaquin aimed center of mass and squeezed the trigger. The man staggered backwards, dropped his rifle and clutched his chest. As he fell, he was lost in the forward surge of hundreds of men.

Joaquin heard the other Rangers firing their rifles along with him into the crowd. The screams of injured and dying, the yelling of scared and angry men rose above the mass movement of bodies. Those to the rear tried to surge forward and those in the front attempted to turn and retreat.

Joaquin saw that a few of the men had actually crossed Chase Creek, and one was struggling with Elliott. The man had hold of Elliott's rifle, attempting to take it away. Together, they wrestled for control of the rifle. Elliott's back momentarily turned toward the miners.

Joaquin's breath caught in his throat—a large powerfully built man ran toward Elliott with a club in his hand. Without thinking, Joaquin brought his rifle up and pulled the trigger. *Nothing happened. Oh my God, I'm out of ammunition!*

He watched with his mouth open as the man closed the gap toward Elliott, the heavy club swinging. Panicked, Joaquin dropped his rifle and ran toward the assailant, still unable to yell out a warning to his friend. As he sprinted forward, he instinctively drew his six-shooter and fired almost point blank. The heavy pistol bucked in his hand as he fired once, twice ... as fast as he could cock and fire. The .45 slugs caught the man in the chest high up, and in the neck, blood erupted from his throat. Elliot twisted the rifle away and shot his other attacker.

Suddenly the rain was pouring down on them with all semblance of visibility gone. Wheeler ordered the Rangers back up the road from Chase Creek where they formed a new skirmish line.

The rain continued in torrents. Lightning flashed and thunder resounded in the distance and then, BOOM, it was upon them. The skies opened up and it seemed to Joaquin as though hell came with it. Walnut-sized hail pelted then battered them; rain deluged them. Each man ran for some kind of cover from the punishment as the lightning lit up the dark skies and thunder boomed like cannons directly over them. Men no longer cared about combat, only of saving themselves from the storm. Joaquin heard a noise. A loud moan? No, more like a—roar. It got louder the longer he listened. Then he saw it. A huge wall of water! It plunged and cascaded down Chase Creek toward them, six or eight feet high encompassing the entire width of the narrow canyon.

Unable to speak, he stared at the spectacle in front of him, his jaw dropped open. Then he forced himself to yell out to Elliott nearby. "Elliott! Look!" and pointed at the oncoming wall of water.

Elliott shouted, "Git back from the crick, boys! Move!" Elliott started to run then stumbled and reached for his right knee. The rest of the Rangers scrambled back from the creek bottom. Joaquin ran to Elliott, grabbed his arm, and pulled him to higher ground.

The miners were not so lucky. Sheets of rain continued. Lightning and thunder reverberated off the canyon walls. Those at the front near the creek bed had no way out. The wall of water roared through the narrow canyon, sweeping bodies down stream. The men left standing as the huge wall of water roared past them scrambled uphill to high ground and the safety of the lime pit.

After retreating to high ground, the Rangers held their secondary skirmish line. Water surged up to where Joaquin was standing, overrunning his boot tops. He stood his ground, leaning against a boulder near the road. Trembling as he reloaded his rifle and his handgun, he had difficulty holstering the pistol. Suddenly he tasted bile in his throat; then he vomited, several times. His face felt numb. After a few moments, he began to breathe easier. Joaquin took off his hat, closed his eyes and with his head turned up toward the gray cloudy sky overhead, let the soothing rain wash his face and run in rivulets slowly down his neck and onto his shirt collar.

Joaquin took a deep breath, regaining his composure. *Oh, my God.* He swallowed hard, again tasting the residual bile in his throat. *I've killed a man. Please forgive me, Lord.* He looked at the raging creek below him; debris appeared then disappeared in the churning, foaming brown water. *Carmen, it's going to be a long year. ¡Te amo! I love you!*

CHAPTER EIGHTEEN

Tim Campbell moved cautiously from one step to the next at the front of the old schoolhouse, his wooden crutches maintaining his balance. He grasped a small cotton bag tightly in his right hand. It was recess time and he couldn't wait to get outside with the other children. He had grand thoughts of using the marbles in the bag to beat all contenders on the field of play.

He approached a group of boys who had just started to play marbles. A circle had been drawn in the dirt with a stick, and the boys had all their prized marbles out to begin play. Tim swung his crutches forward, then his feet and legs. He dropped the crutches and sat down near the circle.

One of the older boys yelled, "Hey, watch it! You almost hit me with them things."

Tim's face reddened, he dropped his head. "Sorry, Bruce. Can I play marbles with you fellas?" He started to open his bag of marbles.

Bruce looked him up and down with a smirk. "We don't need no cripples playin' with us. Go on. Git!"

One of the other boys spoke up. "*Hey*, Tim can play with us."

"Thanks, Joe." Tim reached for his marbles again.

Bruce ignored the other boy and stood up, towering over Tim. Tim looked up at him. "I have a right to play same as you ... and I'm *not* a cripple."

"The hell you ain't. Why, look at you ... with your leg and foot all shriveled up and having to use them crutches."

"I'll tell you this only once, Bruce. Don't think you're going to bully me anymore. My Dad told me it's best not to fight, but to not cotton to any more woolin' from you. So, back off."

Bruce looked down at his seemingly easy prey. "You're a liar, too, you little cripple. You ain't got no dad. Everybody knows that."

"Yes, I do. And he's the best dad anyone could ever have!"

"You goin' to git—or am I goin' to have to move you?"

Joe pleaded, "Leave 'im alone, Bruce. I mean it."

Ignoring Joe once again, Bruce reached down and roughly grabbed Tim's shirtfront. Simultaneously, Tim reached down and picked up one of his crutches. As he was lifted, Tim brought the crutch straight up as hard as he could. The hard wooden crutch hit Bruce under his chin, knocking him back to the ground with a thud. He yelped in pain and surprise. Holding his chin and mouth, Bruce struggled to get up. Tim grasped the crutch firmly in both hands and swung at his adversary with all the strength he could summon. The crutch arched around from his right side and hit Bruce alongside his head sending him sprawling away from the group of boys. The bully lay there holding his head, his eyes dazed and his mouth bleeding. Then he began to cry.

Tim looked around the circle at each of the boys then at Bruce. "You had enough?" The bully did not answer and continued to cry.

"Do the rest of you mind me playing with you?"

Joe laughed. "You goin' to whack us all up side the head if we say no, Timmy?"

"No, I don't want any trouble ... just want to play is all."

He turned to his tormentor still lying on the ground holding his head. "You ever touch me again or call me a cripple; I'll bust your head so hard you won't be able to think for a week."

Joe grinned and looked across at Tim. "You want to play marbles or not?"

Tim scooted up to the circle again and took his marbles out, laying them carefully on the ground in front of him. He then picked up his best, most favorite marble, placing it on his right thumb held there by his forefinger. He was ready to ... how did Elliott say it? Remembering, he smiled broadly. He was ready to "clean their plow."

Thank you, Dad...for everything. As he let the marble fly at its intended target, he imagined the old Ranger saying, "Wel-l-l ... ya done alright, boy. I'm right proud o' ya."

CHAPTER NINETEEN

It was shaping up to be a long day, and Joaquin didn't feel like talking. He wasn't eating much either; he fought down the nausea whenever he thought about the gunfight. *I killed a man.*

Although the flood had saved the small force of Rangers from the overwhelming crowd of angry miners, it thoroughly ravaged the mining town of Clifton farther downstream from Morenci. Harry Wheeler went back to headquarters at the hotel with Captain Rynning and Sheriff Parks.

Joaquin heard Chapo Carter grumbling to Elliott again about the detail, "This here jest ain't right. Hell, we're Rangers fer Christsake!"

Frank Shaw chimed in, "I agree with Chapo. Besides, most of these workers ought to be getting what the Whites get in wages—'course they shouldn't be rioting."

"I heerd ya." Elliott paused. His blue eyes bored into each of the men standing beside him. "Rumor has it weapons are cached in certain houses throughout town." He removed his hat, scratched his head. "We're to help Jim Parks' deputies conductin' house-to-house searches."

Elliott assigned Wade, Joaquin, and two deputies to enter a specific house and conduct the search. Elliott, Carter, Shaw, and Hopkins remained outside to prevent anyone from interfering with the search inside.

The ancient adobe house served as a residence for a Mexican family. The rusty screen door hung loosely from the front of the house. As Wade moved it aside and knocked on the door, it creaked and nearly fell from the single hinge holding it in place.

Joaquin stepped to the opposite side of the door away from the front of the house. He heard Elliott talking to one of the neighbors, the Mexican man was yelling that they had no right to search any of the homes.

Wade pounded on the door and shouted, "*¡Abran la puerta!*"

The door opened slightly, a frightened face appearing from behind it. Wade lowered his shoulder and slammed into the door. The man who was standing behind it reeled backwards. Wade, Joaquin, and the two deputies then charged into the room. The Mexican man in his thirties pushed a woman behind him.

Quickly, Joaquin surveyed the darkened room and saw three small children huddled on a metal frame bed in the corner of the room.

One of the deputies ducked out the back door, looked outside and said, "Nothin' out back, Bill ... just desert."

In his best Spanish, Wade advised the man they had a search warrant and asked if he had any firearms in the house. When the man did not immediately respond, Wade grabbed his shirtfront, drew his six-shooter and shoved the barrel into the man's mouth and repeated his demand, "*¿Tiene armas?* You damned greaser bastard." The frightened man was unable to speak.

Joaquin saw urine spilling from the front of the man's pants onto the dirt floor.

Wade said, "I ain't got time fer this ... you boys tear this place apart an' see what you can find." He turned and slammed the pistol barrel hard against the man's head. Joaquin heard a sickening hollow thud as the heavy revolver struck the man's skull. The man slumped to the floor, blood pouring from the wound. The woman screamed and crouched on the floor where the man had fallen.

One of the older children screamed, *"¡Papá!"*

During his search, one of the deputies found an old single barrel 12-gauge shotgun. He held it up, hollering across the room to Wade, "Well, lookee here, Bill. These Messicans done got themselves a gun."

Wade looked at the shotgun. "Figgers 'bout right—greaser sumbitches. Keep lookin'."

He reached down and grabbed the woman by the hair, pulling her to her feet. "What else you got? Huh, bitch? Speak up!"

Joaquin had been unable to speak or act with all the events unfolding in front of him so quickly. He forced himself to move next to Wade. "Bill, there ain't no call for this. Let her go. I'll speak to her."

"What? The greenhorn Ranger knows what's best? You—who's still wet behind them ears?" Wade turned to Joaquin, still holding the woman by her hair.

"I'm just saying ... we don't have to hurt 'em is all."

"Boy, you need some larnin' bad. These here greasers will cut your throat or shoot ya in the back in a heartbeat. You best larn thet or you'll be one dead Ranger!" He roughly shoved the terrified woman at Joaquin. Joaquin caught her in his arms and almost fell backwards.

"Maybe ya otta search her ... huh, boy?" sneered Wade.

Joaquin responded hotly, "Bill, what I'm saying is they're not all bad people. *Mexicanos* are like everybody else—some good an'" some bad."

"You don't know jack 'bout nothin', boy." Wade snarled.

"Enough to know that I'm marryin' a nice Mexican gal."

"You *what?*" Wade's mouth gaped, his eyes wide.

"You heard me. She and her father are fine people, better than some Whites that I'm looking at."

"You watch your mouth—or I'll shut it!" Wade moved toward Joaquin. His voice changed, soothing, "I'm just lookin' out fer ya boy, thet's all."

The deputies finished their search of the room without finding more firearms. Joaquin helped the woman carry the fallen man over to the bed next to his children.

"I'd never would o' thought o' ya bein' a Messican lover, boy."

Joaquin didn't respond to the taunt from Wade. He only felt sad and sickened that he had been a part of something he knew was wrong. He knew in his heart they could have conducted the search and found the shotgun without violently attacking the family. Bile rose in his throat once again.

Joaquin's squad searched ten houses in their section of town, and they found a substantial number of firearms. It was enough to warrant the Rangers' concern. Two of the Mexican miners assaulted them during the process, and they were arrested and hauled off to jail. Other Rangers and deputies searching other sections in town also found firearms. The confiscated firearms included double barreled guns, revolvers, and shotguns of all types.

That evening while Elliott and Hopkins met with the command staff to discuss future plans, Joaquin's squad walked down the street to a saloon located near the hotel where they were staying.

Carter's boots dragged on the board sidewalk. "I'm plumb tuckered." His voice was low, full of weariness.

Shaw agreed, "Me, too. It's been a long day." He pulled his hat down. "Just glad none of us got hurt—or killed."

Wade, Carter, Shaw, and Joaquin sat at a table in the dimly lit, smoke filled saloon. Wade ordered a bottle of whiskey and glasses for all. He poured each man a glass of whiskey, placed the cork back in the bottle and set it down on the table.

He then raised his glass. "By Gawd, here's to the Arizonie Rangers boys an' each one o' ya."

Joaquin watched them raise their glasses and toss the whiskey down their throats. Then he took a swallow. The whiskey burned his throat then worked its way down to his stomach. He coughed, but somehow managed to keep the whisky from coming back up and out his nose.

Frank Shaw, next to him, leaned over. "Warms your belly, don't it, Joaquin?"

Joaquin coughed again. "Wow, it sure does!"

Wade uncorked the whiskey bottle then peered at Joaquin. "Drink up boy. We're ready fer another round. I kin see thet I need to edjicate ya fer shore." He reminded Joaquin of a banty rooster back home on the ranch.

Chapo Carter pushed his glass toward Wade. "Fill 'er up agin Bill. And while you're at it, leave the boy alone. I don't reckon he needs your kind o' lessons."

"Why Chapo ... I'm plumb hurt by thet." Wade feigned a hurtful expression on his face while pouring another round of drinks. He softened his voice to Joaquin. "I jest thought we'd have a few friendly drinks together an' celebrate us bein' Rangers and all." He downed his drink. "Why, Joaquin here kin drink or not with us, I reckon. Don't matter to me none. Just tryin' to be friendly is all."

Joaquin swallowed the rest of his glass of whiskey. This time it was easier, and it made him feel warm and relaxed. He pushed his glass over toward Wade. "I appreciate that, Bill. Gimme another one of them if'n you would. Please, sir."

"Why, it would be mah pleasure, boy. Welcome to the Rangers." replied Wade jovially.

Joaquin had several more drinks of whiskey. He felt both happy and melancholy at the same time. He knew he was getting drunk and it was time to head back to the hotel, but somehow he allowed the men to cajole him into staying and having another drink, then another. As he sat slumped back in his chair half asleep, he heard Bill Wade say to someone from behind his chair, "Take this—you better take proper care of 'im upstairs. You try to take his money or any o' his things, I'll beat the hell outta ya. Now go on ... help 'im up."

Joaquin felt someone take hold of his arm and help him stand up. He smelled perfume and felt a soft touch. A woman stood next to him, supporting him.

She smiled at him. "Come on, honey. Beth will take good care of ya." She led Joaquin to the rear of the saloon and then up the stairs. They entered a small, dingy room, and she helped him onto a small cot. He felt her fumbling with his clothes and he squinted to make out her features in the dimly lit room. He felt his pants being unbuckled and then pulled down and off his legs. After a few moments, he felt the woman fondling him. Then he felt her astride him and saw her large pendulous breasts in front of his face. As he suddenly realized what was about to happen, he lunged to one side, pushing her roughly onto the floor.

"Hey! What the hell?" She struggled up from the floor as he swung his legs over the edge of the cot. It was all he could do to keep from being sick. He lowered his head between his knees. The woman came around the bed and stood directly in front of him. He glanced at her, taking in her nakedness. He dropped his head again.

With a surprise tone, she said, "Look here mister, I know you're ready for a poke, an' I ain't too shabby to look at—what gives?"

"It's not your fault, ma'am." Joaquin said. "It's just ... well ... I ... I'm gettin' married to a gal back home."

"You *what?*" Then she threw back her head and laughed a throaty laugh.

Joaquin rubbed his hands over his numb face. "Is there

a back door out of here?"

The woman gazed at him. She turned, walked around the cot to where her clothes were strewn on the floor, and began to dress. "Yeah. The door in the corner leads to stairs that go down behind the saloon." When she finished dressing, she brought his clothes and helped him dress. "You won't tell Bill we didn't do nothin', will ya?"

Forcing bile back down his throat, Joaquin struggled to speak. "No. I'll tell him that you was a good poke, ma'am."

"Thank ya. If'n he finds out otherwise, he'll beat me ... *bad*."

"I understand. He'll never know from me."

She helped him stand and walk out the back door and down the flight of stairs to the darkened alley behind the saloon. "Will ya be alright gittin' back to the hotel? You don't look so good."

"Thank ya, ma'am. I'll make do."

"All right then ... I best be gittin' back to the saloon." She laughed, "You know—customers waitin' an all." She started up the stairs then turned. "I hope thet gal you're fixin' to marry knows what kind of man you are. I'm bettin' she don't have no idea. Most women don't appreciate a good man even if they're lucky 'nough to have one. That's why most of my best customers are married men. I reckon I've knowed less than a handful of really good men in my whole lifetime." She sighed, frowning. "What did you say your name was?"

"Joaquin."

"Joaquin?" Her hardened eyes softened. "Well, Mister Joaquin ... the world's a better place for you bein' in it, I'd say." She walked briskly up the stairs.

The next day the Arizona National Guard showed up in Morenci, two hundred thirty strong under the command of Colonel James McClintock. It was a good thing for the

Arizona Rangers as most of them were hung over from the previous night. A day later two hundred eighty cavalrymen from Forts Grant and Huachuca arrived. Everything appeared under control, and Governor Brodie decided the Rangers could return to their regular duties within the territory.

On June 11, the Rangers gathered, preparing to leave by train from Morenci. Rex Rice, manager of the local Phelps-Dodge Mercantile approached them.

"We sure appreciate all you boys done for us quellin' the strike." Rice shook hands with each Ranger. Then he asked, "How about a picture of all o' ya?"

Elliott was quick to respond. "Naw, I reckon not."

Captain Rynning spoke up, "I don't see any harm in it, boys." He gestured to the men. "Come on—get on over here."

Carter mumbled, "Aw Cap'n, do we hafta?"

"Yes. It's an order," answered Rynning.

Reluctantly, twenty-three of the Arizona Territory's finest lawmen lined up in a single-wide row and had their first and only group picture taken.

Joaquin Campbell posed proudly, holding his .30-.40 Winchester rifle at his side. Next to him stood his friend and mentor Elliott, a newly built cigarette hanging out the corner of his mouth with his left leg supporting most of his weight. Only Jeff Kidder, the newest member, who was tending the Douglas office, was absent from the historic photo.

CHAPTER TWENTY

C armen Ponce lifted the heavy lid of the cast iron cook stove after inserting the metal handle. She carefully placed kindling mixed with larger wood inside, lit it, and watched the fire grow. Satisfied it was burning readily, she replaced the heavy lid. As she turned away from the stove, she looked out the window. The few clouds left over from the previous day became a pale pastel of pinks as the sun rose in the east over the Whetstone Mountains. She hoped the summer rains would begin soon to cool the temperatures and replenish the parched desert with much needed moisture.

Carmen was dressed for work in riding boots, pants, and a blue cotton jumper, and her long black braids hung down over her shoulders.

She rolled the *masa* and patted it between her hands, the way her father had shown her years ago. Would she teach her children the same tradition? Ranch life was all she knew, but she also had an inkling of another kind of life, the one her friend Megan Campbell lived. Carmen often thought being a teacher might be something she would like to do. But would the "powers that be" even allow her to attend the Teacher's College in Tucson as Meg had done?

Sometimes she felt she had no feminine side, as she was mostly around men. Carmen had never known her mother, who had died giving birth to her nineteen years earlier. She was glad for Marion and Megan's company. It was nice to do "women things", wear a dress and feel like a woman. She loved her father more than anyone, even more than

Joaquin, only in a different way. But after all, *Papá* was still a man. And Joaquin—where was he now? She prayed to God every night before she went to sleep that he would remain safe and return to her. It was up to God now ... Him and Joaquin.

Carmen wanted to marry Joaquin more then anything in the world. *Por Dios.* She had thought of nothing else since she was a little girl. She knew with all her heart and soul that she loved him dearly. She wanted to be his wife, the mother of his children ... and yet? Would she ruin his life by doing so?

She could only imagine the difficulties that lay ahead for an Anglo man married to a Mexican woman. She was not immune to comments, the insolent stares and the "looks" from some folks in the community. She could not bear to think their children would be mistreated, or even have to endure what she herself had endured already. Would they be considered "half breeds," a term she had heard of others' heritage? In her culture they would be less, "*cuarterones*" —quartered ones!

Light began to shine through the kitchen windows as the day brightened outside. Carmen finished making the tortillas and added more wood to the fire. A shuffling, scraping sound at the door to their two-room residence announced her father as he stepped into the room carrying a bucket of milk. He set the bucket on the table and gave Carmen a long hug. "*Buenos dias, mi'ja.*" He smiled. "*¿Como amaneciste, luz de mi vida?*"

"*Muy bien, Papá. ¿Y tu?*"

"*Bien, mi'ja. Gracias a Dios.*"

Carmen smiled and told him how special he was to her as well. *Papá's* hair had turned snow white within the past year, and the long scar alongside his head was always prominent. *Pobrecito—so close to death that day.* Sometimes, mostly in the evenings, Domingo became melancholy and sad. Carmen knew he was thinking of his friend. It was the time when he and Lou sat on the porch smoking, visiting, or just enjoying the quiet together. Carmen had done her best to fill that void, but it was just not the same.

She felt badly for Marian Campbell as well. Marian had always been her *madre* and the older woman treated her as her own daughter. Carmen vowed to never forget that kindness. And Joaquin? The murder had changed the course of his life, and in doing so, it had changed her life as well. She admired him for being so adamant that his father's killer be brought to justice. But she feared his insistence on being a part of Chacon's capture would get him killed. He was so young and naïve in a world full of bad people.

Her father had told her many times he thought the Rangers were finally making headway in cleaning out the bad element. Men like Elliott.

How she loved the old Ranger. He had always been so kind and gentle to her. He and her father were close friends, trailing herds of cattle, then helping to settle the new Arizona Territory. She had never been afraid of Elliott, but she had seen the violent side of him on several occasions and was well aware of his reputation as a tough, hard man. She knew he had a dark side to him that he did not want her to see. *God, please help Elliott keep Joaquin safe so he will come back to me.*

Solo Vino barked outside, startling Carmen. Her father reached for the Winchester rifle leaning against the wall near the door, and stepped outside onto the porch to see what Joaquin's dog was carrying on about.

Carmen followed. Several men on horseback rode toward the ranch dwellings. The dog continued barking and the horses in the corral began to get excited, running around inside the circular enclosure constructed of ocotillos interlaced together. Then she recognized the tall slender man sitting the saddle so easily on the *grulla* horse.

"Elliott! Viento!" Behind them she saw the paint horse and Joaquin leading a pack mule. Her heart raced. Behind the first two, trotted three more riders and two additional pack mules. *Thank God, they're okay.* She held her hand to her wide-open mouth, and she started to run to Joaquin. She stopped herself, stood on the porch. *No. That won't do …*

The Rangers pulled up to the hitch rails near the corral. Marian Campbell came out of the main ranch house, waved and smiled at Elliott. "Howdy, stranger. Glad you dropped by to see us."

Elliott dismounted, removed his dusty old hat, and slapped it against his leg. "Marian, your shore a sight fer these ol' eyes. How are ya?"

"Why, I'm fit as a fiddle, I reckon. You boys want some breakfast?"

Before Elliott could answer, Joaquin dismounted and ran over to his mother, hugging her, lifting her off the ground. He looked her over; a bright smile appeared on his face. "Would we *ever.* Elliott's a fair cook, but it ain't nothin' like your home cookin', Mom."

"Well, git yourselves unpacked and them horses cared for 'an come on over to the house. You're all welcome at my table."

"Thank ya, Marian," replied Elliott. "We'll not be spendin' the night. We've got to git on the way to Douglas, but we'd shore appreciate a hot meal." He turned toward the other men as they stood near their horses. "We'll share a meal here with these folks an' then head out." He stepped to his horse, threw the stirrup over the saddle, loosening the cinch.

He spoke softly to Joaquin. "You'd best git over there and tend to thet pretty 'lil gal standin' on the porch, boy. I'll take care o' your hoss."

Joaquin stared at Carmen then he hurried to her, his spurs jingling. *He's here ...really here ... with me again.* Her pulse quickened and her eyes glowed as he hugged her, nearly squeezing the air out of her lungs. She returned the hug.

He had changed somehow, but she could not put her finger on it. Thinner than she remembered. His deeply tanned face with a few days beard stubble looked more mature, more serious maybe? His range clothes were covered with dust as was his hat. When they embraced, she felt a revolver beneath his jacket on the left side. Didn't Elliott carry a second revolver in a shoulder holster? Well, no matter. She was so happy to see him again and to know he was all right.

She smiled up at him. "You look well, Joaquin."

Another voice near them startled her. "You don't look too bad yourself 'lil lady."

She turned toward one of the Rangers, dressed in black clothing with a dark swarthy complexion, and a full handlebar mustache extending out beyond his face on both sides.

He stepped in closer and looked her up and down. "You ain't a bad lookin' filly atall. I kin see why the boy has takin' a likin' fer ya ... Messican an' all. Why, in mah day ..."

Joaquin's sharp voice interceded, "That's enough, Bill!"

The man's voice had an edge to it. "Don't git all riled up, boy. I kin mind mah manners when I'm bein' shown hos-pi-tal-ity. Ain't ya goin' to introduce me to your sweetie here?"

"This is Carmen Ponce. We're going to be married."

"So ya said, boy ... so ya said—just the other day as I recollect."

"Carmen, this ... is ... Bill Wade," Joaquin said between clenched teeth.

Carmen felt the hair on the back of her neck bristle.

There was something about him she did not like, something ugly ... evil ... that made her feel very uncomfortable.

She put her hand out and attempted to smile. "It is a pleasure to meet you, *Señor* Wade." As they shook hands, she felt a revulsion that almost made her jerk her hand abruptly away, but she somehow kept herself from doing so.

Joaquin stepped in between her and Wade placing his arm over her shoulders. "I'm starving for home cookin' ... let's eat."

Carmen met the other Rangers over breakfast. Bow-legged Chapo Carter, who seemed like many a cowhand she had met over the years; sincere, hardworking, and not one to talk much. Frank Shaw, the young Ranger who hailed from Kansas and was not much older than Joaquin. He was a tall, slender, nice looking man with dark brown curly hair and an easy smile.

These are good men. With Elliott and these two men, surely Joaquin will be safe.

After they finished eating, the men built their cigarettes and drank more coffee.

Elliott leaned forward on the kitchen table. "Marian, how's the ranch work goin'?"

"We're makin' do—me, Domingo, 'an Carmen. No complaints. What have you boys been up to?"

Elliott drew on his cigarette; smoke exited his nostrils. "We're goin' to Douglas then we'll be headed down to Mexico after Chacon within the week."

"It's about time. If you don't get 'im soon, he'll be back up here—up to his old tricks again."

"I reckon you're right. We'll git 'im. I promise ya thet." He stood. "Well boys, we'd best be headin' on out."

They all got up from the table, expressed their thanks

for the meal and began filing out the door toward their horses. Before he went out, Elliott asked, "How's Meg an' Timmy doin', Marian? They okay?"

"They're both doin' well. Thanks fer askin'." She stood next to the table. "Maybe if you was to be in Douglas fer a few more days, she could come over and see ya?"

He smiled briefly, his brown leathery face wrinkling, "I don't want to put her out none, Marian, but it shore would be swell to see her." He paused. "Well, you take care now an' don't work too hard. See to it thet Domingo an' Carmen don't neither."

Carmen watched the line of riders disappear from sight. Her lips quivered then parted. She knew she had to be strong not weak, especially now with Joaquin headed to Mexico and into certain danger. She headed to the barn, caught her bay gelding, brushed him down and saddled him. There was a lot of work to be done and her father depended heavily on her. She sighed deeply as she brushed away a tear that began to run down her cheek. *Our Father who art in heaven, hallowed be thy name ...*

She snugged up the cinch, led the horse outside, walked him for a few minutes then further tightened the cinch. Her father had saddled his horse and stuck a rifle in the scabbard attached to his saddle. As she watched him mount his horse, she saw he was wearing a pistol belt with a cross-draw holster; a heavy .45 single-action revolver was encased in the worn holster.

Oh, my God, what has become of us?

CHAPTER TWENTY-ONE
July, 1904

M egan Campbell leaned forward in the saddle. The rain that had collected in the recesses of her wide-brimmed hat spilled out onto the saddle horse's neck and mane. Her knees ached from being in the saddle for so long. Dismounting to walk for awhile, she couldn't help thinking how worried she was about Timmy—*he'll be okay with Mama*. Should she have taken this trip alone? It was already taxing her strength. She was cold, wet, miserable—and anxiously nervous. Was it all worth it? The answer was always the same for her. *Yes, I love him so! But can I really do this?* The rain slicker, leather chaps and tapadero stirrups were a Godsend; they protected her for the most part from the incessant torrents of rain.

Mama had packed provisions in the saddlebags and Domingo had her father's horse saddled and ready when she arrived at the ranch to switch out horses. She truly wanted to see Elliott and Joaquin before they left for Mexico to hunt down Chacon.

Megan's stomach growled. She checked the saddlebags for the provisions her mother had packed for the two-day trip. She ate jerky and dried fruit, mounted again. *I have to find some kind of shelter before nightfall.*

She pushed the gelding hard, reaching the outskirts of Fort Huachuca just as dark was approaching. She decided to make camp in the desert out of sight from the road. Under the shelter of a large mesquite tree, she built a small fire. It was a cold wet night and she didn't sleep well. *The wind ...*

blows and howls so. I'm so lonely and afraid.

Megan lay in her wet blankets, shivering, cold—waiting for the dawn that seemingly eluded her grasp. Then the dark sky gave way to light; she could see well enough to ride on. *Thank you, God!* She arose; happy to finally start a new day, and rode all the way to Bisbee, boarded the horse at the stable, and obtained lodging at the Copper Queen Hotel. She had been so exhausted she slept all night and into mid-morning the next day.

Upon awakening, she washed her face and then her hair in the washbasin provided, changed clothes, and ate breakfast at the hotel. As she stood from the table, she saw a bearded man seated at a table next to her, staring. She looked again in his direction; he continued his insolent stare. *What?* She was quite aware it was unusual for a woman to travel alone, but this attitude? *You rude ... no, don't swear, Meg.* She turned away, tossing her hair. *Ha! Take that, buster.* She had absolutely no interest in what anyone thought, only of seeing the men she loved. She paid the stable fee, quickly saddled the sorrel and headed out at a brisk trot for Douglas.

As she made the descent from the Mule Mountains range and Bisbee, the clouds began to break up and occasionally the sun shone, warming her as she rode along. She sang *How Great Thou Art* then hummed the tune. The higher elevation vegetation of scrub oak and pinon pine mixed with grassland gave way to the true Sonoran desert landscape. Megan rode easily in the saddle, oblivious to aches and pain. She would be there soon. The bleak desert floor was inundated with greasewood, mesquite, palo verde, and ironwood. Large ocotillos prominently extended up above the smaller greasewood plants with their numerous green leaves amongst the thorny branches, brightly displaying that it was indeed the rainy season. Later, the ocotillos would drop all their leaves in order to survive the hot dry desert environment. She reined in the sorrel. *I love this beautiful country—it's so special to me.*

Once on the desert floor, Megan spurred her mount into an easy lope, and rode for about a half-mile then dropped the horse into a trot. She figured that she had at least twenty miles to go before reaching Douglas. The rain had let up with intermittent sunshine. Her tack and gear was drying out and she had tied the yellow rain slicker behind the saddle. She thought of what her father had told her many years ago and laughed; her laughter resonating out in the quiet desert landscape. He had said that rain slickers were worn out most often from being tied behind the saddle and dragged through the brush rather than when a cowpuncher actually wore the darn thing.

Megan pushed her mount hard for several hours. Looking to the east, she could see smoke at several locations spiraling up toward the upper atmosphere and numerous buildings that appeared to be play house size. *Thank you, God! I've almost made it.* As she rode on, Douglas and its sister town Agua Prieta across the border in Mexico loomed larger. In the distance, the Perilla Mountains east of Douglas helped break up the monotonous flat desert floor.

She had been to Douglas once before with her father, and she knew from first hand experience that it was a rough border town. Saloons, gambling houses, and bordellos lined Tenth and Sixth Streets. These included the Cattle Exchange, the Waldorf, and the White House. Men played faro, poker, roulette, and other games of chance as painted harlots sang and danced before a raucous crowd of lonely men starved for feminine attention. Drinking, prostitution, and gambling were the order of the day in the dusty border town.

Her father had told her the most notorious honky-tonk in Douglas was the Cowboy Home Saloon on rowdy

Sixth Street where murder, robbery, and deceit were as common as men spitting tobacco into the spittoons along the bars.

As Megan rode into the western outskirts of town, she saw the numerous tents and buildings that had been constructed for the new Phelps Dodge smelter that appeared to be almost completed. She continued down the main thoroughfare, G Street, past the large Phelps Dodge mercantile store and other two-story brick structures that had sprung up along the main street in town. These buildings were in stark contrast to the predominant low flat-roofed adobes that comprised most of the structures throughout Douglas.

Reaching the south end of town near the Mexican border, Megan reined her horse onto Fifteenth Street and sighed with relief when she saw the small Ranger Headquarters building just down the street. Exhausted and sore from all the hard riding the past several days, she only hoped she was not too late and the long hard journey had been for nothing.

Elliott concentrated on repairing a sawbuck packsaddle sitting on the top rail of the corral behind the Ranger Headquarters building. He heard a horse trotting nearby and then a familiar whinny. *Sounds like Lou's sorrel hoss.* Turning, he saw a woman riding the familiar horse toward him. His jaw dropped open. He could not believe his eyes.

He started to speak then stammered, "Meg? Is thet you? What the heck are ya doin' here, gal?"

Megan swung down from the horse and almost fell. Elliott sprang forward and grabbed her.

She took in a deep breath and exhaled slowly. "I'm so glad you're still here, my friend. I was afraid you had already left for Mexico."

He held her out from him, surveyed her from head to toe.

"Wel-l-l now ... ya come all the way over here to see Joaquin an' me off did ya? I'm plumb tickled Meg, an' I know your brother will be when he sees ya. He and some of the others are gettin' supplies in town. I reckon he'll be back shortly."

"I—I'm so glad, Elliott." She stepped back to him and hugged him with all her might.

He returned her hug with equal enthusiasm. "Meg, ya gotta be plumb wore down to the nub with thet long ride. Let me put your hoss up in our corral, an' I'll git a buggy down here to take ya to the Gadsen Ho-tel. How's thet ?"

She stepped back and laughed out loud. "I would truly appreciate not having to ride horse back for awhile." She took off her hat and shook out her hair. "I must look dreadful."

"No, I reckon not. Meg, you're the best lookin' thing I've seen in a long while."

She blushed, averting her eyes.

"Let's git ya inside an' Sergeant Hopkins kin set up a buggy ride fer ya. I'll take care of your hoss," he said.

She bit her lower lip then returned his stare.

He lowered his eyes and stammered, "Meg ... I ..." He hesitated, swallowing, "I ain't much fer words—never have been."

She smiled, placed her arm in his as they walked toward the Ranger Headquarters building. She said softly, "We'll talk later, my friend."

Sergeant Hopkins arranged for the buggy to transport her to the Gadsen Hotel located just east of G Street in Douglas. She found the accommodations to be excellent and the hotel clerk very informative as well.

"Yes ma'am, this hotel is one of the finest in the territory. Take those beautiful marble stairs leading up to the rooms.

Why, the infamous bandit Indio Chacon rode his horse up those stairs once. See that chipped portion of the stairway? Then he shot holes in the ceiling with his six-shooter and rode off into the night."

"My word ... a horse—in here?"

"Yes ma'am. Exciting times that's for sure."

Elliott and Joaquin showed up in the lobby as planned and the three of them had supper at the hotel restaurant. Megan enjoyed being with the men, listening to them talk of the ranch, family, and the impending Ranger sortie into Mexico in pursuit of Chacon and his band. After dinner, they sat together at the table, and the two men each drank a shot of tequila and Megan enjoyed a glass of wine.

Joaquin stood. "Well, I think I'll turn in. We head out in the mornin' for Mexico." He sighed. "To be honest Meg, I want to be done with it."

"I know. We all want it finished. You be careful, listen to Elliott, and come back safely—you hear?"

"You bet, Sis." As she stood up, he reached forward kissed her on the cheek and hugged her tight.

They heard his spurs jingling on the board sidewalk.

Megan and Elliott sat at the table enjoying the quiet. Megan finished her wine, stood and walked around the table to Elliott. "Let's go talk somewhere quiet, shall we?" She reached out her hand to him.

He rose and hesitantly extended his hand to her. Fumbling money out of his pocket, he left it on the table for the meal. They walked out of the restaurant and up the marble staircase of the lobby.

At her door, Elliott hesitated, staring at the floor. He paused before speaking. "Meg ... it ain't ... proper fer me to be in your room."

Unlocking the door, she took a deep breath and looked up at him.

"Do you love me, Elliott?"

He did not hesitate but frowned slightly, "Yes. I do love ya, Meg ... more'n a man should, I reckon."

"But ..." she said.

"Its jest the ... well, mah wife an' boy ..."

"They're gone from this life, Elliott. You still have a life to live. I would like it to be with me. I love you so!" She hugged him, laid her head against his chest, and swiped the tears that flowed down her cheeks.

Tenderly stroking her soft brown hair, he whispered, "I know Meg, but it ain't easy to let go."

"I'm not asking you to let go of those you love, only to share yourself with me—here and now—in *this* life. My father always told us kids that each of us has our time in the sun and to make the most of it everyday."

He shuffled his feet uncomfortably. "I'm gittin' old, Meg. Hell, I am old! Why, I reckon I've been around way more'n half a century." He shuffled his boots. "Thet an' I ain't been with a woman fer a long time ..."

"I'll be forty years old next month." She let her statement sink in. "I'm no spring chicken myself. It's been a long time for me too, Elliott. My husband's been dead for many years."

She pursed her lips, wrinkling her brow. "I guess what I'm saying is that I'm more than willing to take a chance. I can honestly say that I love you unconditionally, and I want you in my life."

She leaned closer and whispered, "As fer the skedoodlin' part, *ah reckon* we'll do just fine together." She smiled.

He couldn't help but grin as he held her out at arm's length. "Megan darlin', I reckon you're right at thet. Will ya marry this ol' man if'n he kin make it back from Mexico?

"Yes. But I'm not asking that from you."

"Well ... I am! Thet's the deal, take it or leave it, *'lil missy*."

She laughed, not answering right away. She smiled again. "Since we're talking of marrying, what ... exactly is your first name? I've only heard you referred to as Elliott, nothing else."

"I reckon Elliott is as good a handle as any, Meg."

"Seriously, what *is* your first name?"

He hesitated, toying with his mustache then said, "Samuel T., bein's it's you doin' the askin'." It was his turn to smile, his tanned face breaking into wrinkles. "I reckon I don't hafta tell ya thet 'lil bit o' information ain't fer no one but you."

Before she could answer, he pulled her close into his arms, bent down and kissed her fully on her lips. Hungrily, he pulled her tightly to him and kissed her again, this time more passionately. She surprised him as she returned his kisses with her arms around his shoulders and neck. He pressed against her. Wanting her to feel his urgency, he held her even more tightly, breathing heavily. He saw her face flush with mounting excitement.

She reached out and took his hand as she hurriedly shoved the door open. Fumbling, they somehow managed to get inside the room. Megan closed the door softly behind them.

CHAPTER TWENTY-TWO
Mexico, August 1904

awd, its hot ... hotter'n ten rats in a damn wool sock. Elliott laughed at the thought and wiped his neck and face of perspiration with his red handkerchief as the noonday sun beat mercilessly down on him and the others. Massive saguaro cacti dotted the Sonoran desert landscape. He reined up his horse as a Gila monster lumbered between several rocks nearby. The hideous black and orange creature stopped and looked back over its shoulder at the approaching strangers. Then it seemed to shrug and continued ever so slowly on its journey through the hot, desolate desert.

Elliott had led the Ranger contingent out from San Bernardino Springs, crossed the border into Mexico, and started down into the San Bernardino Valley. The six Rangers rode in single file with the newest in their ranks, Joaquin Campbell, at the rear leading the four pack mules fully loaded with provisions and ammunition to sustain them for the mission that lay ahead.

Captain Rynning had worked out the details for their sortie with Governor Yzabal of Sonora, Mexico and the infamous Colonel Kosterlitzky of the Federal Rurales. The Rangers would be allowed to enter Mexico, conduct their operation to find and arrest Indio Chacon and his outlaws wherever they were located in the Sierra Madre Mountains. Since Colonel Emilio Kosterlitzky insisted that at least two Rurales ride with the Rangers, they were to rendezvous with the Rurales near the confluence of the San Bernardino and Bavispe Rivers.

Elliott had worked with Kosterlitzky on several occasions in the past. He found him to be a hard dangerous man, but the times called for such a man in Mexico. Elliott was well aware that Kosterlitzky, a former Russian Naval cadet who had jumped ship and joined the Mexican Calvary, was a brilliant, remarkable man, fluent in nine languages. He had worked his way up through the ranks until he was top man in the Rurales, no easy task.

Elliott figgered they should make it to the confluence the next day, hopefully around noon, but they had some hard riding to do in the meantime. He turned in the saddle and hollered to Carter, "Chapo—take drag, will ya? I don't want them mules to drop way back from the rest of us."

Carter nodded to him and reined his bay horse off to the side, allowing Joaquin and the pack string to move around in front of him.

Elliott touched his spurs to Viento, and the horse broke into an easy trot. The horse turned his head to eye his master. Elliott broke into a broad smile.

"Yep. I know ... no point in gittin' all lathered up too early on this here trip. We mostly likely got us a good eight days or more 'afore we find thet bastard."

His grin faded as he thought about what lay ahead on this dangerous trip into Mexico. Hell, dealing with Chacon was bad enough, but they could easily cross paths with the Yaqui Indians and other bandits on their way down to the Sierra Madre Mountains.

Salty perspiration trickled down his face and irritated his eyes. He remembered the terrain and the lay of the valley as he rode south. It'd been awhile since he'd been down this away. How long now? Christ, must o' been in 1883 with General Crook. The "old man" they had called him out of respect. Elliott still had vivid memories of those days, some twenty years ago.

After joining the Army, he had become good friends with one of the Chiefs of Scout, Merijildo Grijalva. At age ten Grijalva was captured by Chiricahua Apaches. At age eighteen he escaped and fled to an American fort. By 1866 he served the U.S. Army as a scout and interpreter.

Grijalva liked Elliott because he never met another man until he met Elliott who hated the Apaches more then he did and who killed them with a vengeance at every opportunity. Eventually Grijalva persuaded General Crook to allow Elliott to ride with the scouts, the first and only Anglo to do so.

Elliott's band of Rangers today was small in comparison to the '83 expedition into the Sierra Madres. He recalled Chato, Bonito, and Geronimo had stolen cattle and horses in Arizona and New Mexico then run to Mexico. The "old man" had finally worked it out with the Mexican government to allow a total of 235 scouts and soldiers to track the Chiracahua Indians into Mexico. It was the first time American troops had been allowed into Mexico to chase Apaches, and Elliott had been more than ready.

Elliott left his past behind and concentrated on the present as the Rangers camped along the San Bernardino River drainage that night. He had the men take turns guarding the horses and mules as well as their camp throughout the night. They couldn't afford to lose any men or any of the horses and mules to thieves. They rose early and rode into the fertile Bavispe River Valley.

Elliott pulled his horse up and studied a small adobe house several hundred yards south of the confluence, up the Bavispe River. He first saw the confluence many years ago. *Why, it warn't nothin' but desert ... no farmin' like now. Too damn many Injuns in them days, I reckon.*

They were to meet the Rurales there, according to Kosterlitzky, but Elliott was taking no chances. He surveyed the house, barn, and corral with his field glasses. Half a dozen horses milled inside the corral. Two saddled horses and an unsaddled pack mule were tied to the corral and saddles, blankets, and various tack hung on the rails.

Elliott rotated the glasses to take in the old adobe house itself. Smoke spiraled straight up from the chimney. He studied the surrounding terrain.

Turning in the saddle, he advised the Rangers behind him, "Ever'thing looks fine to go on in, but I want Chapo an' Bill to ease on around to the back o' thet house. Then the rest of us'll ride in the front side."

Carter and Wade nodded and spurred their horses into a trot.

Elliott swung his right leg over the saddle horn, pulled his tobacco and papers from his shirt pocket and built himself a smoke. He figgered they had come more'n fifty miles and had maybe six days or so to reach the old Apache *rancheria* that he believed Chacon was using to hide out. He'd received good intelligence a year ago of the location, and he recalled riding into the encampment chasing after Geronimo and the other Apaches. Finding the hideout wasn't the problem. The problem would be gettin' into it without being seen or ambushed.

Elliott wiped sweat from his forehead. *Damn it's hot! A man can't even enjoy a cigarette.*

He finished his smoke, swung his foot back into the stirrup and looked through his field glasses once more. Carter and Wade had completed their wide berth around from the northeast and were almost behind the house.

"It's time to see if'n them hosses belong to Rurales or a bunch o' no good bandits." He and the three other Rangers rode up the river bottom toward the adobe house.

As they approached the front, Carter and Wade did likewise from the rear of the house. As instructed, Joaquin held back from the others with the mule pack string as Elliott and two Rangers fanned out in front of the house. A man of Mexican descent stepped out the front door, followed by two other men. All wore wide sombreros with high peaked crowns, and all were armed with revolvers. The first man out the door walked toward the Rangers resting his hand on his holstered revolver.

"*Señores ... ¿Quién son ustedes?*"

Elliott dismounted, placing Viento between him and the man, leaving him out in the open with no cover. The other two Rangers in front dismounted and took cover behind their horses as well.

Elliott called out, "Arizona Rangers ... *¿y ustedes?*"

The man took his hand off his gun and grinned broadly. "*Bueno*, I am Arturo. I work for Emilio ... I am with the Rurales." He looked directly at Elliott. "You—you are *Señor* Elliott ...*¿Qué no?*"

"I'm Elliott. I was told to meet up with Arturo Gomez. You him?"

"*Si, Señor.* We are all Rurales here. These two men will travel with ..."

He whirled as Bill Wade appeared from behind him, his six-shooter in his hand. One of the other Mexicans stepped between Wade and Gomez. Wade brought the heavy .45 revolver up and sideways across the man's face, knocking him to the ground.

His nose bleeding, the dazed man struggled for his handgun. Wade then placed his boot heel against the man's throat as the man clawed for his revolver; Wade kicked him hard in the face and took his pistol from the holster throwing it out and away.

"Goddamn greaser bastard. Good riddance, I say," snarled Wade, as he waved his revolver at the other two Mexicans.

Elliott stepped around his horse and shouted, "Put your

gun up, Bill! What the hell do ya think you're doin'?"

Joaquin dropped the lead rope on the pack string and spurred his paint horse straight at Wade, hitting him from the side, knocking him down. Wade lost his grip on the revolver. As he started to get up, looking for his gun, Joaquin leaped from his horse directly on him shouting, "*¡Pendejo!*"

He hit Wade hard in the mouth with his fist as he straddled him. The heavier man easily threw Joaquin off to the side and stood up, wiping blood from his mouth. He looked again for his gun, but Elliott had it tucked in his gun belt with his own revolver leveled at the two other Rurales.

Wade snarled at Joaquin. "You 'lil Messican lover. You'll regret what you just done. I'll beat ya bad fer this."

Joaquin rose to his feet. "You worthless *son-of-a-bitch!* All you ever do is beat or kill Mexicans! I'm ashamed to be a part of the likes o' you. Why do ya hate 'em so bad— huh?" Joaquin gasped for breath. "You're part Mexican ain't you, Bill ... is *that* it?

"You 'lil bastard. *I'll kill you!*" Wade charged Joaquin. Joaquin stepped easily to the side as the big man surged past him and hooked a blow behind the man's ear, sending him reeling sideways.

"You had 'nough, Bill?" Elliott drawled.

"No! Not till I whip thet 'lil bastard," shouted Wade, breathing heavily.

"If'n I was you ... I'd let it go," said Elliott sharply.

Elliott turned to Joaquin. "You kin finish it *mi'jo*, but I reckon I'll take your pistol first." As Joaquin tossed his revolver to him, Elliott turned to Gomez. "These two kin finish this ... then we'll talk. Don't be reachin' fer them pistols o' yours. "*¿Comprende?*"

"*Sí, Señor* Elliott. And you have some explaining to do. Please allow me to help my friend."

"You go ahead." Elliott looked at Chapo Carter standing near the house with his revolver drawn. "Chapo, you cover Arturo and his friends. I'll make sure this here's a fair fight."

Wade had recovered his breath by now, and without waiting he moved toward Joaquin. He circled the younger man slowly. More cautious now, he clearly had the advantage in experience and size, and he knew it. He had been in many a brawl over the years, and he had won most of them. He moved in closer and threw a punch straight out toward Joaquin's face. His mouth dropped when his adversary parried the punch easily to the side with his open hand.

He threw a left-handed jab quickly followed by a right hand for Joaquin's jaw, missing contact with both. Then he charged forward, clasping the smaller man in a bear hug. He smashed his head against Joaquin's nose and forehead— once, twice—and brought his knee up hard toward Joaquin's groin. Joaquin struggled to free himself from the grasp of the heavier man, and managed to turn slightly deflecting the knee strike. Blood poured down his face from his nose and he felt light-headed.

Wade released the bear hug, grabbed the front of Joaquin's shirt with his left hand, and cocked his right arm and fist back.

Joaquin grabbed Wade's left hand with both of his hands and stepped backward, pulling the heavier man off balance. With Wade's thumb down Joaquin held the wrist stationary with his left hand, and used his right hand to drive Wade's hand abruptly up and against the wrist joint. Wade screamed in pain as he was driven to his knees.

Joaquin kicked him hard in the face several times while holding the wrist and hand stationary. He felt Wade weaken, and he let go of the man's wrist and arm. Joaquin gasped for air and could not see well due to the smashing blow to his nose. He summoned all that was left of his strength as he balanced on his left leg and kicked up and sideways with his right leg. As his leg extended, his boot heel caught Wade fully in the mouth, his spur raking the man's face and the blow propelling Wade backward to the ground. Wade rolled to the side and then collapsed, unconscious. Joaquin staggered backward.

"Easy, *mi'jo* ... easy. Ya beat 'im, fair and square. Li will be proud 'o ya," Elliott shouted in his ear as he helped him stand.

The Mexican Arturo stood from caring for his fellow Rurale. "*¡Que bueno!* You have been taught well, my young friend." He turned to Elliott. "This young rooster fights with a fury, *Señor* Elliott."

"Well, Arturo ... I reckon a man's got to let the badger out now an' agin."

Arturo's face had a puzzled look. Then he threw back his head and laughed loudly. "*Sí, Señor Elliott. El tejón ...tiene razon—*you are right." He paused, peering at the unconscious Wade. "And now ... what happens?"

"The way I see it this changes nothin'. I'm sorry fer the way Wade acted. There wasn't no call fer it. But you kin see thet he got what he had comin'. I'd say we're even." Elliott led Joaquin over to the porch of the adobe house where he helped him sit down. "How's your friend, Arturo?"

"I'm afraid that he has a broken nose, cannot see out of one eye, and will be of no use to you in the field."

"Kin ya take Wade back to the border without shootin' him along the way?"

"I would do us all a favor by putting a bullet in his brain right here, right now, *Señor*."

"Thet may be so, Arturo, but I don't cotton to murderin' folks. I'm a sworn peace officer ... same as you, *Señor*. Will ya give me your word thet no harm will come to him if'n I leave him with ya to take back?"

Arturo let out a long sigh. "You are expecting a lot, *Señor* Elliott."

"Jest call me Elliott. I don't need no fancy handle in front o' it. Lookee here Arturo, I'll send a telegram to my Captain at the next town. I garntee ya thet he'll be wherever you say at the border to pick up Wade. And I'll see to it thet Wade's punished fer what he's done here, but I need to go on down 'an git Chacon. *Now* ... not later. Let me take your other man with us. We'll be short on officers, but I reckon we'll make do."

Arturo shook his head as he pursed his lips. *"Sí.* I give you my word that I will not allow this pig to be harmed. Further, my other *compadre* is at your service."

"Muchas gracias, Arturo." Elliott turned to Joaquin. "You goin' to be alright to head south? We're burnin' daylight, boy."

"Yessir. I can make it."

Elliott handed his pistol to him. *"Bueno.* Git them mules then and see if'n ya kin set your hoss." He paused, gesturing to Frank Shaw. "On second thought ... Pancho you pull them mules fer a spell. Let's git movin'."

As the other Rangers and the newly acquired Rurale mounted for the trip ahead, Elliott led Viento over to Bill Wade, where Arturo covered him with his revolver.

Sitting now, Wade spat blood then a tooth from his mouth. "Don't be leavin' me here with these greasers. They'll gut shoot me jest as soon as you're outta sight."

"No. I reckon not. Arturo's given his word not to harm ya. He'll take ya back to the border. I'll have Wheeler meet ya there. He kin do what he wants with ya, but ya ain't riding with me no more."

"Don't leave me here, *Goddamn you!"*

Elliott mounted his horse and joined the others waiting for him. He touched his spurs to Viento, who broke into a trot, and reined him south. There were two fewer men than the original plan had called for, and Joaquin could barely sit his horse. Six men—five Arizona Rangers and one Mexican Rurale—headed up the Rio de Bavispe Valley toward the forbidding Sierra Madres.

Wade's impassioned screams and blasphemy echoed up the canyon following the men, replaced by an ominous silence.

CHAPTER TWENTY-THREE

S hortly after daybreak, Joaquin was wide-awake. He got up, washed his face in the river, and retrieved his wooden toothbrush from his saddlebag. While reaching for his tin of salt, he heard someone walking up from behind. He turned to see Elliott, hatless, his hair white as the driven snow.

Joaquin smiled and murmured, "Howdy, Elliott. Mornin'."

"Well, howdy yourself, *mi'jo*." Elliott gestured toward Joaquin's old wooden toothbrush. "If'n you're fixin' to brush them teeth boy, try some o' this here goop." He tossed a tube at Joaquin, who dropped his tin of salt as he caught the object. He looked closely at the tube in his hands.

"They call it toothpaste. It beats hell outta using salt or baking soda," proclaimed Elliott. "Damned if it don't have a kinda peppermint candy taste to it. It ain't half bad. Go on, try it."

Elliott pulled his tobacco "makins" from his shirt pocket. He built himself a cigarette and lit it. Drawing deeply, he blew soft rings of smoke that mysteriously hesitated, then floated out and away from him.

Joaquin squeezed the paste hesitantly on his brush, wet it with water from his canteen, and begin to gingerly brush his teeth. He smiled broadly at Elliott, and spit out a mouthful, "This stuff ain't half shabby. Why, it does taste like candy; almost anyways and you're right, it sure beats hell outta using salt."

Elliott returned the smile, "You keep thet new fangled goop, boy. I got me another one o' them in mah saddlebags."

"Thanks."

Joaquin thought about what lay ahead for the days to come. They had left the adobe house three days ago, riding hard and camping at night along the Bavispe River drainage. Elliott sent a telegraph message to Ranger Headquarters in Douglas from the Mexican village of Bavispe. He told Captain Rynning of the altercation involving the Rurales and Arizona Ranger Bill Wade and that the two Rurales were bringing Wade back to the border at Agua Prieta.

Joaquin shook his head in disbelief over Wade. *Hells bells, they should've turned him over to the Rangers by now.*

After Bavispe, the Rangers and Rurale rode farther up the river valley, passing Higueros Canyon and on through another Mexican village called Bacerac. They were currently camped above Bacerac. Joaquin could see the foothills of the Sierra Madre Mountains in the distance, and he knew they were getting that much closer to their quarry.

"If'n you're through shinin' them pearly whites, how about packin' them mules standing oe'r yonder. We're burning daylight." Elliott chuckled as he walked away.

Joaquin repacked his toiletry items and walked over to one of the mules. Reaching down, he picked up the saddle blanket with one hand and the sawbuck packsaddle with the other. He placed the saddle blanket up over the neck and withers then slid it back a few inches to smooth out the hair on the mule's back, and swung the packsaddle onto the center of the blanket.

He spoke gently to the mouse colored jenny mule, "Easy now, Francis ... just gotta cinch ya up tight, ol' gal."

He flipped the double cinches and breast collar from the packsaddle to the other side of the mule. Joaquin stood at the mule's left shoulder just out of reach of her hind leg and grabbed the cinches as they swung under her belly. He laughed as she tried to "cow kick" him.

Pulling the latigos through the cinch rings, he cinched the saddle up tight. Standing next to the mule, he pushed the britchen harness over its back and rump, and reached around in front and connected the breast collar to the cinch ring.

Frank Shaw, who was saddling one of the other mules, turned to Joaquin. "Gimme a hand with loading this sumbitch, Joaquin, and I'll help you load Francis."

Joaquin stood on the off side of the mule facing Shaw. He lifted his fully loaded canvas pannier just as Shaw did on the opposite side, and both hooked the heavy leather straps over the wooden "sawbuck" portion of the saddle, positioning equally weighted loads on either side of the mule's back.

Elliott walked past them, and Shaw asked him, "How many days do you reckon before we get to Chacon?"

Elliott paused. "If'n I recollect right, we got to git on up the Rio Bavispe an' go through Hauchinera. Thet village is 'bout ten miles from where we're camped. From there it's maybe twenty-five miles to the village of Tesorababi." His boot probed the loose, sandy soil at his feet. "I reckon thet's near the head of the Rio Bavispe. Then we'll be up in them Sierra Madres, boys."

Shaw yelled, "Headache partner!" and tossed the heavy cinch and rope over the pack load toward Joaquin, who stepped back out of the way to avoid being hit in the head. Joaquin stepped forward, centered the rope over the pack load on his side, and swung the cinch underneath the mule's belly toward Shaw.

Joaquin said to Elliott, "What was it like in the days when the Apaches were here—and thicker than hair on a dog's back?"

"Well ... a man had to be mighty careful if'n he wanted to stay alive."

Elliott built a cigarette and lit it. Shaw snugged the pack rope tight over the load. Quickly, he threw a half hitch over the open end of the cinch to ensure that the rope stayed taunt then threw the remaining rope over the pack to Joaquin.

Elliott withdrew the lit cigarette from his mouth. "We'll hafta be more careful from here on. Chacon will most likely have folks watching out fer 'im."

He drew again on his cigarette and exhaled. "You was askin' what it was like; there warn't no farms like we been seein' here along the valley. And them Mexicans was scared to death of the Apache ... had a right to be, I reckon. They was fierce proud warriors in them days. In the '83 trip, I remember goin' through the village of Nacori."

Elliott pointed in a southerly direction indicating the location of the village. "The whole damn place was pert near wiped out by the Apache. I recollect only three hundred folks left alive and outta them maybe only fifteen men an' boys. Why, I reckon ever' Mexican family lost two or more folks killed or captured by them Apaches."

Joaquin finished tying the single diamond hitch on top of the pack. He asked, "The Apache must have been a tough bunch to tangle with in those days, huh?"

Elliott reached back in time. He tried to toss the distressing thoughts aside, but he couldn't. He remembered all too clearly the battle at Skeleton Cave, high in the Sierra Madres, some twenty years ago. The very same place he was leading the Rangers to capture the bandit Chacon.

It had been bitter cold that day. *Colder'n a well digger's butt.* The Army Scouts found the Apaches easily, living in the cave. Chief of Scouts Merejildo Grijalva led the scouts directly to the rancheria. He had been there many times as a captive and then a member of the Chiricahua band.

He positioned twelve to fifteen sharpshooters on the hill

above the cave. Elliott was one of the sharpshooters. They sneaked up on the encampment undetected and caught the Apaches off guard. After all, no one had ever pursued them into the mountains of Mexico. No one knew it at the time, but it was the beginning of the end for the Apache.

The hidden sharpshooters shot twenty warriors at the outset of the battle. The others—men, women, and children—retreated inside the cave. From there, the warriors fired at the Army Scouts from behind boulders at the entrance to the cave. Grijalva then ordered the Scouts to pour all their firepower at the cave walls inside. Ricocheting bullets killed indiscriminately. Twenty warriors charged the sharpshooters from inside the cave and were savagely cut down just yards from the cave entrance. The Scouts kept shooting into the cave until the enemy failed to return fire.

Elliott and nine other volunteers charged into the cave, killing the wounded warriors on their way inside. What he found inside the cave had sickened him. There were twenty more dead warriors and thirty-six women and children, dead or dying on the cold cave floor.

He found a young Apache woman, who had been shot in the stomach. He knelt beside her, seeing the fear and agony in her widened, shocked eyes. She was clutching her dead child, still trying to protect him.

The Hualapais and Yavapai Scouts were smashing the heads of the dying Indians with rocks. One scout approached the woman. He raised the rock above his head. Elliott pointed his rifle at him and yelled for him to get away from her. He told the scout if he came back to harm the Apache woman, he would track him down, shoot him, and crush his head with a rock.

Elliott guarded the woman closely and made sure that no one harmed her. Making sure that all the other scouts had left the area, he gave her his canteen of water and all of his rations. He collected dry wood and cached it inside the cave for her. Then he built a small fire close to her to keep her warm. With her permission, he buried her dead son back in the deep recesses of the cave.

During all his preparations for her, she looked at him strangely. He thought maybe she didn't understand the kindness being shown what with all the savagery and butchery just moments before. When it was time for him to leave, he gazed down at her for several minutes. He felt honestly good about what he had done for her, thinking that if only years ago someone had done the same for his wife and son. *Damn, it's a hard world thet we live in.* He sighed deeply, thinking of his dead wife and son, pushing back the tears. Then he turned and walked outside to his waiting horse.

That day had forever changed him and his seething hatred of the Apache. Shortly after the battle, he resigned from the Army and began drinking heavily. He became very proficient with his gun and hired out to almost anyone for his killing skills. Although he wanted more than anything to be killed, he found no one who could best his deadly skills with a gun.

Elliott felt the cigarette butt burning his finger, and he dropped it quickly to the ground, breaking his bond with the ghosts of the past.

"Elliott? You all right?" queried Joaquin.

"Shore ... I'm fine, *mi'jo.*"

"We're all packed up and ready to travel now."

"*Bueno.* We'd best be movin' on, I reckon." Elliott sighed as he walked over to his *compadre,* Viento. He saw the others were mounted and ready to ride. He swung easily into the saddle, reining in his frisky mount.

He looked at the Mexican Rurale mounted beside him. "Carlos, ride up front with me. I want Carter and Joaquin in the middle. Butler, you pull the pack string. And Shaw, you ride drag and watch our backs. From here on we've got to be ready fer trouble. If'n we ain't, it'll be our bones bleachin' out in the hot sun with them damned Apaches from the past."

CHAPTER TWENTY-FOUR

C armen rode her bay horse slowly toward the barn. Lightning flashed overhead, momentarily lighting up the overcast skies, and seconds later the expected thunder boomed, spooking her horse. He pranced sideways and reared. As she brought him under control, rain poured down on them and her view of the barn in the distance was obscured. *No le hace. The horse knows the way. Por Dios. I'm so tired tonight.*

The rain continued to pelt her, running down the brim of her hat and off her rain slicker. A bad day for her, weatherwise. She had traveled up Cienega Creek to check on the cattle to the north. Several of the cows were calving and her father wanted to ensure that both cows and calves were healthy. A thunderstorm caught her by surprise and her clothing was soaked before she could don the rain slicker. The wind then chilled her clear to the bone.

The bay horse stopped suddenly.

Carmen leaned forward in the saddle and peered through the heavy rain. The heavy barn doors loomed in front of them. She sighed in relief and dismounted, feeling the water in her boots squish as her feet touched the ground. Opening the barn door, she led her horse into the dry warm interior out of the pouring rain and driving wind. The rain pelted the tin roof of the barn like hail.

She tied up the bay, removed her rain slicker, untied the latigo and unsaddled. As she lifted the wet saddle and blanket up to the corral pole inside the barn, she thought she heard a shuffling sound. "*¿Papá?* Is that you?" No one answered. She strained to see inside the darkened barn. As her vision adjusted, she saw a black horse tied in the far corner. *Whose horse? Who was ...?* She had seen the black before. She was sure of that, but when? BOOM! Thunder cracked overhead startling her. *My God, I am so tired. What am I shaking for anyway? Time to get to the house.* She turned to walk back toward her horse.

"Well, if it ain't thet purty 'lil Messican what Joaquin wants to marry."

Carmen whirled toward the voice coming from directly behind her. A man wearing black clothes and boots and a wide-brimmed black hat stepped out of the shadows in the corner of the barn. He stopped within a few feet of her, and she made out a large handlebar mustache. *Who? Oh yes* ... the Ranger that she had met several weeks ago and had taken an instant disliking to.

"I remember you. You're one of the Rangers."

The man studied her before answering, "Yup. Bill Wade's the name."

"What are you doing here, *Señor* Wade? I thought all of you were in Mexico hunting Chacon?"

The man snorted a laugh. He stepped closer.

Carmen knew she should turn and run, but she couldn't. A shiver went through her entire body. Ice ran through her veins.

"Thanks to your goddamned Joaquin, I ain't goin' to be a Ranger no more," he snarled.

Finally able to move her feet, she turned and ran for the barn door. Wade caught her before she made it. He grabbed her by the hair and roughly dragged her back to the center of the barn. Her bay horse reared, trying to break free.

She screamed, and he grabbed her by the throat with his right hand. "You scream all you want, you little bitch.

No one's goin' to hear you none in this here storm. Besides, if'n your ol' man comes in here, I'll kill 'im." Wade grinned broadly, "Hell, I might jest kill 'im anyways, jest like I done them Mexican Rurales down in Mexico tryin' to turn me in."

Carmen stopped struggling, and he relaxed his grip on her throat. She quickly aimed a kick at his groin, but he twisted his body and took the blow on his leg.

"Why, you 'lil greaser bitch, you'll pay for thet. I'm gonna beat you ... real bad!" He spat in her face. Cocking his fist back, he hit her hard in the mouth, knocking her to the ground. Then he kicked her hard.

It seemed to Carmen he would never stop kicking and hitting her. Her vision blurred, and her face and ribs were racked with a sharp, intense pain. It was like a horrific nightmare, an experience that was not really happening to her, but she knew for certain with each jarring blow that it was.

As she faded in and out of consciousness, she heard him say, "I ought to cut your goddamn throat with this here knife by Gawd, but I want thet bastard Joaquin to see ya hurt real bad and to hear from you what happened."

Carmen felt him cutting her clothes, then ripping her blouse and pants from her body. The cold permeated her body. She felt sick to her stomach. Blood trickled down her face and she couldn't see out of either eye. Her face felt numb. She choked, coughed and spit blood. *Oh, my God. How can this be happening? I've ... got to get up ... run!*

She attempted to struggle once again.

"I ain't done with ya jest yet, greaser bitch!" Wade hit her again in the face.

Why does he hate me so? What have I done to deserve this? My God ... my Savior ... please let me die. I can't endure much more of this... She knew she needed to fight, to run, but she had no energy or ability to do either. He roughly jerked her legs apart and began his final assault on her.

Carmen prayed. *Our father who art in heaven, hallowed by thy name...*

CHAPTER TWENTY-FIVE

L ieutenant Harry Wheeler stepped down from the trolley in front of the Capitol Building in Phoenix, Arizona. As he made his way into the ornate building and up to the Governor's office, he couldn't help but worry about the upcoming meeting. Captain Rynning had asked for help from him in responding to the Legislators' proposal to abolish the Arizona Rangers.

Wheeler shook his head in disbelief. How could anyone living in the territory not understand what the Rangers had accomplished the past four years? Hell, all the sacrifices made—a good Ranger killed in the line of duty and undoubtedly more to die so the lawlessness would cease and citizens might live in peace.

Wheeler ascended the stairs and walked down the long corridor toward the Governor's office. He stopped in front of the door and slapped at the dust on his suit jacket and pants. Finally satisfied that he looked presentable, he knocked on the door and entered without waiting for a response, removing his hat.

Governor Brodie stood and approached Wheeler with a broad smile on his face. "Harry, how are are you, my friend?" He shook Wheeler's hand with a firm grip. "Come in ... come in. We were about to begin our discussion."

Wheeler quickly surveyed the room. Three men sat at a table adjacent to the Governor's desk. Across the table from the three men, he saw two chairs, one occupied by his boss, Tom Rynnning. The Governor motioned for him to sit down in the unoccupied chair next to Rynning.

"*Hola, Tom. ¿Como estas?*"

"*Bien, gracias. ¿Y tu?*"

One of the men seated at the table leaned toward the two Rangers. "We don't need no Mex talk at this here meetin'."

Before either of the two Rangers could respond, Brodie glared at the man and said, "That's enough, Thomas." The Governor cleared his throat. "Well ... gentlemen. Allow me to make the necessary introductions." He motioned to the three men across the table from them.

"The gentleman on the far right here, who doesn't ... speak Spanish ... is Legislative Councilman Thomas Weedin."

The stocky older man appeared to be in his late fifties. His salt and pepper beard distinguished his hard face and his mostly white hair hung down to his shoulders. He wore a dark suit with a tie and the jacket was opened, showing an expensive gold watch chain along his closed vest. On the table to his left were a large white sombrero and a dark stained walking stick. Weedin nodded curtly to the two Rangers but said nothing.

Wheeler thought, *what the hell is this guy up to? He's gonna be trouble for us.*

"And adjacent to Councilman Weedin is Councilman Brady O'Neill of Maricopa County."

"It's a pleasure to meet two of Arizona's finest." With a quick smile, O'Neill extended his hand and shook hands with both Rangers. He had a boyish face but appeared to be in his thirties. His brown hair was slicked back and his handsome face was smooth- shaven. He wore a dark suit and tie with the shirt collar turned up, one of the newer fashions of the day. His gray Stetson hat lay on the table with the crown down and the brim up.

Smooth ... too much so for my liking.

The Governor continued with his introductions. "The gentleman on your far left is none other than Representative Sam F. Webb."

"Howdy, boys. Good to see ya," replied the older man. He was dressed similar to the other politicians, but carried himself differently than the other two men. He appeared to be an outdoorsman and a very down-to-earth type of individual.

He's an old cowpuncher—that's good for us, but what does he want?

Brodie turned to the two Rangers and introduced them to the politicians.

Governor Brodie sat behind the large desk. He took out a cigar then tossed the box to the center of the table. "Help yourselves, gentlemen!"

Brodie lit his cigar, drew deeply on it, and exhaled. "I called this meeting to discuss any issues that you gentlemen may have in regard to the Arizona Rangers. And I have made available the two men who run the outfit for any specific questions I can't answer."

He puffed on his cigar, waiting for the others to light theirs. "I want to point out I've heard from certain sources ... that each of you men apparently have concerns. If this is indeed true then let us allay those concerns or issues today, here and now."

"We don't need a bunch of men settin' around campfires drinkin' coffee 'an doing the same work our local peace officers do," growled Weedin.

Governor Brodie looked at Rynning. "Tom, you want to respond to his statement?"

"Yes sir. Councilman Weedin, we have proven our usefulness many times since the Ranger company was created. Our Rangers patrol mostly remote areas. These areas are almost never traveled by local peace officers, but are haunts for outlaws and badmen."

Wheeler spoke up. "Sir, the company rode over 10,000 miles horseback this past year, an average of 390 miles per man. Over the last four years we've arrested numerous rustlers, murderers, rapists, horse and cattle thieves, and as you men know, we played a large role in containing the violence from spreading during the labor dispute at Morenci."

Councilman O'Neill leaned forward in his chair. "Tell me, Captain Rynning. Why do you men spend so much time ... how should I say it ... being livestock inspectors?"

"We've worked hard at eliminating the rustling problem here in the territory, sir. As you know, it was out of control in 1901 when we ..."

"Yes. I am quite aware of that," interrupted O'Neill. "I believe that job should be paid for solely by the cattlemen, not general taxpayers of the territory."

"And another thing," interjected Sam Webb, "why are the Rangers devoting so much time looking for smugglers on the border? Hell, that's not what we hired you boys to do."

Rynning shifted in his chair. "We do assist the line riders on both sides of the border, sir. These smugglers are the *same* individuals who are committing heinous crimes of murder, rustling, grand larceny and theft."

Thomas Weedin looked contemptuously at both Rangers. "I understand you boys contribute a part of your salary to the Republican Party, isn't that so?"

"What did you say? Rynning stood.

"You heard me," retorted Weedin.

"The answer to your question is—*no*." He fought to maintain control of a rising anger. "We have *never* contributed monies to either party; Democrat or Republican, and I resent this line of questioning, sir!"

"Easy, Tom," Governor Brodie soothed.

O'Neill leaned back in his chair, obviously enjoying

the moment. "I think its common knowledge the Ranger company was created by a Republican administration and is regarded by most of us as a Republican instrument here in the territory."

"We're not here today to discuss party politics, gentlemen. Let's stick to specific questions about Ranger issues," said Brodie.

"Hell bells, Brodie," exclaimed Webb. "Every damned county in the north is agin ya. You don't have nary a ranger stationed up yonder."

"You're right, sir," returned Captain Rynning. "And we intend to correct that shortly. Up to now we've pretty much worked the southern part of the territory because most of the problems have existed along the border with Mexico. However, we plan to extend our rangers up north with a northern detachment stationed out of Flagstaff, St. Johns, and Fredonia."

Weedin stood, placed his hat on his head and picked up his cane. "Well, I've heard enough. One of these days we Democrats will outnumber Republicans in the Arizona Legislature, and then this Ranger issue will be dealt with ... once and for all."

O'Neill and Webb followed.

Lieutenant Wheeler was silent during the previous interchange in conversation. His voice rang out in the still room as the politicians filed toward the door in the Governor's office.

"It appears you men have no idea what the Arizona Rangers are all about, what we have done these past four years, and the sacrifices we have endured for the citizens of this great territory." His jaw was set, eyes flaring. "What troubles me most about all of you is that you're so quick to condemn us for your own political reasons, and you have no interest in truly knowing what kind of job we are striving to accomplish or the problems we are facing."

The men stopped just inside the door of the office.

"And *you* ... Mr. Weedin ... you *dare* suggest that we not speak Spanish in front of you. Speaking a language that nearly all of your constituents, white or brown, speak on a daily basis offends you? You damned ignorant *hypocrite!*"

"Nobody talks to me that way!" roared Weedin, his face mottled purple.

"I'm talking to you that way, you arrogant bastard!" Wheeler fired back.

The three politicians stormed out of the office, the last one slamming the door closed. Dead silence hung in the office.

"Damn, Harry, you sure have a way with words." The Governor's face was solemn. Then he grinned broadly at both Rangers. "Why ... I couldn't have said it more eloquently myself, son."

lliott led the Ranger force undetected around the village of Tesorababi at the head of the Bavispe River. They were getting close to the outlaw's lair, and Elliott did not want to take the chance that someone in the village would warn Chacon of the Ranger's presence.

They followed old trails used for many years by the Apache driving hundreds of stolen cattle, horses, and mules to their *rancheria* high in the forbidding Sierra Madre Mountains. The trail led up one rough mountain range and down another, steep and treacherous with sheer rock cliffs and deep canyons. Slipping or stumbling would mean falling up to a hundred feet and certain death. The steep, rocky canyons made hard going for the heavily loaded pack mules. Elliott had them untie the mules' lead ropes from the "piggin' strings" on the packsaddles when they traveled in the very steep areas of the trail. He figured that way if one mule fell, it would not take the entire pack string and all their supplies with it. The men got off and led their horses along the narrow steep trails.

Frank Shaw had purchased a brand new pair of riding boots before heading down to Mexico. Everyone had trouble walking through the rough, uneven terrain with rocks in their path, twisting their feet sideways unexpectedly. Elliott saw the new, stiff boots were causing problems for Shaw's feet, but there was nothing he could do for the young Ranger.

Elliott had little difficulty finding his way back to the

rancheria. As he rode alone at the head of the column of lawmen, he reflected back on his past life in the Army and his seething hatred of the Apache. He realized in later years he had been terribly wrong to blame an entire people for the actions of a few; however, at the time he didn't allow himself to think that way.

Elliott pulled his coat collar closer around his neck. It was raining intermittently and the wind had picked up. The vegetation, along the ridge tops through the steep, rocky terrain provided some respite from the sharp winds. As they dropped down into a small saddle, Elliott pulled Viento up and turning in the saddle he said, "I reckon we'll make a cold camp here—no fire."

The natural saddle provided a moderately flat area with an abundance of dense piñon and scattered Mexican pine trees. The horses and mules were tied to a picket line and the men fastened oat-filled *morals* or canvas feed bags on the animals. Men and animals would need their strength before the day was out.

Elliott frowned as he watched Frank Shaw remove his new boots and socks gingerly, looking down at the reddened sores and blisters on his feet. "How ya plan on takin' care o' them feet, Pancho?"

"Well, I've been thinking about pouring water in 'em, and letting the water soften up the leather." Shaw paused, wincing. "Dang new boots ... ought to have known better."

Elliott shook his head. *"Buena suerte,* son." He knew Shaw would need more than luck with them boots. Shaw poured water from his canteen into each boot, filling them up past the ankle point.

They were close now, and they all knew it. The men couldn't sit for long and paced back and forth within the cold camp. Chapo Carter rose from the ground and walked to Elliott, standing under a large pine tree. "Shore could use some hot coffee 'bout now."

"Me, too. But I reckon not." Elliott beckoned to the other Rangers. "I'm goin' down the ridge aways 'an see if them outlaws is where I think they are—should only be a mile or two from here. They'll hafta git in and out o' through this here saddle. Keep a sharp lookout. I'll be back shortly." As he departed on foot, he said over his shoulder, "Chapo's in charge."

Elliott disappeared among the trees along the ridge-line. Carter's dark face showed no emotion to Joaquin. "All right boys. Let's git some cold vittles out and eat. I'll take first guard duty. I don't want nobody surprisin' us ... understood?"

When it was Joaquin's turn at guard duty, he chose a location just up from the saddle. From this vantage point, he watched the trail leading toward the outlaw encampment as well as the trail from which they had arrived from the northwest. He figured the site would serve him well at least until dark. He leaned his rifle against a pine tree, reached into the pocket of his wool jacket, and pulled out a dried biscuit. He took a bite and swallowed it down with a drink of water from his canteen. He longed for a stack of hot flannel cakes and a cup of steaming, hot coffee. *But this is better'n nothin'.*

Joaquin looked out over the rugged beauty of the Sierra Madres. *God's paradise, by golly.* He understood fully why the outlaws and the Apache before them had ventured here into the wilderness. The isolation and treacherous terrain kept most others away, which was the way they had wanted it.

These outlaws. They had murdered his father. He clenched his teeth. He would see them hang for what they had done. He fully intended to honor his promise to Elliott. Not murder any of them outright, only kill in self-defense if they threatened to kill him. He had given his word, and that was that.

While he finished eating the biscuit, he studied the two trails again. Something moved below him near the outlaw trail! Scrambling for his rifle leaning against a tree, he nearly dropped it. He peered intently at the location where he thought he had seen movement. To his relief he saw it was Elliott motioning for him to come down to where he was standing beneath a tree. Breathing a huge sigh of relief, he scrambled down the slope.

"Howdy, *mijo*." The old Ranger leaned over and vigorously rubbed his right knee.

Joaquin cradled his rifle in his left arm and pulled his hat down on his head as the wind began to pick up in velocity. "Are they all there, Elliott—where you said they'd be?"

"Yessir, I reckon so." Elliott straightened. "Let's git o'er yonder with them others an' off this here windy ridge." He started forward, stopped and turned to Joaquin. "I reckon ya ain't forgot about your promise to me?

"No sir. I won't murder any one in cold blood."

"*Bueno*. If'n they try to harm ya or anyone of us, why thet's a hoss of a different color."

"I understand."

They walked back along the trail where the other lawmen waited. Elliott had them gather around as he knelt on the ground, smoothing out a wide area. He picked up a stick and drew a line in the ground.

Frank Shaw strode over in his socks, holding his boots. He smiled at Joaquin as he sat down next to him. Then he ceremoniously upended one of his boots. Nothing happened. He frowned, shaking his head in disbelief.

He turned the other boot upside down as well. Again—nothing. He looked closer inside the boots and his mouth dropped open.

Joaquin whispered, "What's wrong?"

"Nothin'." Sheepishly, Shaw hurriedly set the boots behind him, out of sight.

Elliott attempted to suppress a smile. "This is where we're at and the camp is 'bout ... here." He pointed with the stick. "We jest foller this here trail 'bout a mile. The trail follers the ridge line mostly. They got 'em a guard sittin' about ... here, at the cave."

He paused, clearing his throat. "You'll have to take him out quiet-like, Chapo. Chacon's got hisself a nice escape route on 'ther side. He's built a couple o' shacks jest beyond the cave, and his is the farthest one." Elliott pointed out each location on the make-shift map in the dirt.

"I want Carter, Butler, Shaw, an' you, Carlos, to come in the front along the trail, take out the guard and then come on to them shacks. Me an' Joaquin will slip around to the rear and ketch Chacon if'n he tries slippin' out the back way like he's done 'afore."

Carter looked at the map. He rubbed his unshaven chin. "How much time you two gonna need to git in place 'afore we come in?"

"'Bout half an hour, *amigo*. Bein's we'll be movin' slow jest below the ridge an' makin' 'lil sound."

Carter nodded his head. "How many?"

"I seen seven men countin' the front guard, an' three women. I figger there might be ten men altogether, maybe a few more women. Ain't none of 'em expectin' us."

Elliott tapped his stick against his palm. "I figger we'll do better in the daylight. We got us maybe a couple o' hours to git this here job done."

He stood. "We tell 'em who we are and to throw their

hands up. If'n they don't foller a lawful order an' reach fer a gun, shoot 'em. We'll put any prisoners in the cave with a guard when the shootin's over. *"¿Preguntas?"*

Carlos, the Mexican Rurale, spoke up. "It es better to keel all of them now, *Jefe*. It es a *long* way back to the border."

"I reckon you're right 'bout problems watchin' prisoners fer days." Elliott replied evenly. "They might git the upper hand if'n we ain't careful." His gaze bored into each man's face. "But ain't nobody murderin' anybody in cold blood under my command. You don't like them orders then clear out ... *now*. We're peace officers and folks rightly expect more outta us." No one spoke. He looked directly at Carlos. "Kin I count on ya?"

"Sí, Señor. Usted es el Jefe."

"*Gracias*." Let's leave all the hosses, mules, and gear here. Take them spurs off, too. Wind outta help us out today. They'll all most likely be inside. It ain't likely fer them to hear us comin' in—blowin' like it is." He paused. "Let's be safe and shoot straight if'n we hafta. Something happens to me, Chapo's in charge."

Elliott walked over to Viento, withdrew his rifle from the saddle scabbard, and nodded to Joaquin. The two of them walked down the trail and out of sight from the rest of the Rangers.

☼

Chapo Carter pulled a pocket watch from his vest and noted the time. Then he built a cigarette as he watched Frank Shaw working hard to remove ice and water from inside his new boots.

☼

Joaquin followed Elliott as he dropped down off the ridge into the steep rocky outcroppings. It was difficult going and often times it was all they could do to keep from falling to their deaths. He clung to his rifle and moved directly behind the older Ranger. He knew Elliott's bad knee must be hurting him something awful.

They continued traversing the rough rocky terrain, stopping only occasionally to rest. It seemed to Joaquin as though they had been hiking for hours, but he knew it was not so. Finally, they began a slow ascent back toward the top of the ridge. Elliott moved cautiously as he topped out on the ridge using the cover of boulders and vegetation to cover his movement. Joaquin followed suit and soon they were sitting behind a large boulder. Joaquin peeked out from behind the boulder and saw a cabin about fifty yards distant from their location.

"Reckon we're on the far side of the encampment, *mi'jo*," whispered Elliott. He stretched out his right knee, rubbing it briskly with both hands, and leaned toward Joaquin. "If'n Chacon runs once the shootin' starts on the 'ther end, he'll hafta come this away. Ain't no other easy way out. When the Rangers start in on the other side, I'll run to the cabin an' go in fer Chacon. You cover me, wait here—see if'n he slips past me." Joaquin nodded. His heart beat more rapidly. His palms were sweaty.

They sat silent for several minutes. *It's so quiet.* A blue jay sang out in the cool mountain air.

"We don't have long to wait now, *mi'ijo*. You shoot straight, ya hear?" Elliott smiled, his leathery cheeks wrinkling in the sunlight. Then he reached out hesitantly, touching Joaquin's cheek. *Oh, Elliott ... I won't let you down.*

On the other side of the ridge, gunfire erupted and men began to yell. Suddenly, the quiet encampment came alive with men running toward the battle. The air filled with gun smoke as the incessant cold winds muffled the sounds of shooting and screaming. Elliott laid his rifle down, made the sign of the cross, and drew both his revolvers.

Suddenly, he was up and running toward the cabin hold-ing his six-shooters out in front of him. Joaquin watched Elliott reach the front door to the cabin without drawing fire. Elliott leaned heavily against the wall to the left of the door for a moment.

He yelled, "Arizona Rangers. You're all under arrest. Throw your hands up an' come out!"

Almost immediately, Joaquin heard the loud report of shots fired, and he saw the wooden door splinter as heavy slugs tore through it. Elliott stooped low, kicked the bullet-riddled door in and dove through the opening, firing as he entered the interior of the small cabin. Joaquin's heart pounded as he stood up from behind the boulder. He heard several more shots inside the cabin.

He started to run toward the cabin then remembered what Elliott had told him. He stopped, his rifle at the ready. The sound of breaking glass and shattering of wood broke the silence as a man hurtled through the back window of the cabin right in front of him.

A large man, clad in black, hit the ground hard, rolled, and drew his revolver. As he lunged to his feet, he swept a black sombrero from the ground and moved toward Joaquin's position on the ridgeline.

Joaquin gulped. *It's him! It's Chacon!*

He aimed at the man's center of mass, started to squeeze the trigger, stopped and shouted, "Hold it Chacon. You're under arrest—throw your hands up." The outlaw stopped in mid-stride. He dropped his arms down to his sides, but did not drop the revolver.

"*¡Sueltela!* Damn your murderin' hide!"

The man continued to hold the revolver in his right hand. "Yew haf the wrong man, *Señor.* I do not know thees ... Chacon *hombre.*"

Joaquin snugged the rifle firmly into his shoulder. *Watch his hands. His hands!*

The Mexican turned toward the cabin, hiding the revolver behind his leg. Then he raised his left arm.

Joaquin's finger tightened on the trigger. *What's he doin'?*

The outlaw spun, bringing his right hand up to draw a bead on Joaquin.

Joaquin did not remember pulling the trigger, only the recoil of the rifle butt against his shoulder. He brought the rifle barrel back down to eye level, levered another round, and aimed again at his adversary. Chacon fell backwards to the ground, his revolver spinning away from him. Joaquin ran forward with his rifle ready to fire, if necessary.

Joaquin heard shooting in the background and men screaming commands, but he maintained his focus on his enemy. The man clutched his right shoulder, blood seeped through his fingers.

"You keep your hands where I can see 'em." Joaquin stood over the man. This had to be Chacon, but he wanted desperately to be certain of it. "You're Chacon. Admit it!"

The man writhed in pain. "I ... I am not thees ... thees Chacon."

"Say you're him, damn you." Joaquin shoved his rifle barrel inside the man's mouth. "Say it! Or I'll blow the back of your head plumb off!"

The man's eyes opened wide. He attempted to speak around the rifle barrel. Panting, Joaquin withdrew the barrel.

The man spat blood and sat up, still holding his shoulder tightly. Blood was flowing freely down from the wound onto his lap and black trousers. *"Si ... si, Señor. Soy Chacon. Por favor, no me mate."*

"I ought to kill ya. Right here—right now." His hands shaking badly, Joaquin brought the rifle up once again and aimed at the man's head.

Chacon brought his blood-soaked hands up in front of his face. *"¡Ayudame! ¡Por favor, ayudame!"*

Through clenched teeth, Joaquin yelled, "Like you did with my father? Ya yella ... git on your belly. *Now!"*

As the man turned over on his stomach, Joaquin placed his rifle next to him on the ground and reached in his back pocket for the piggin' rope. He dropped down with his knees on the man's back and brought Chacon's hands to the small of his back. Chacon screamed in pain, but Joaquin paid no attention, tying the man's hands securely behind him. Then he rolled the bandit over on his back, opened his shirt near the shoulder and looked at his wound.

Feeling a sudden presence behind him, Joaquin whirled around, drawing his revolver to face the threat.

Elliott stood there looking down at him, smiling broadly. "I been watchin' ya fer a spell, *mi'jo*. And I'm plumb proud of ya." The old Ranger studied the outlaw. "I reckon thet's Chacon alright."

"I still want to kill him, Elliott. Is that so wrong?" Joaquin said between clenched teeth.

"I reckon ya already know the answer to thet or he'd have the back of his head blown plumb off." Elliott sighed then leaned against a large boulder.

Something was wrong. Then Joaquin saw blood on Elliott's shirtfront, blossoming out then dripping to the ground.

"My God, Elliott. You're hurt ... what happened?" He sprang from the ground where Chacon lay and ran to his friend's side.

Elliott grinned weakly. "Ain't nothin' but a scratch, I reckon." He licked his lower lip with his tongue. "There was two men inside the cabin. I shot 'em right off when they fired on me ... then the woman ..." He laughed shortly. "I didn't figger on her havin' a gun." He laughed again, a strained laugh. "Damn good thing she wasn't no good with thet pistol." He stopped talking and sighed again, "I shore hate killin' a woman ... jest didn't have no choice is all."

Joaquin reached for Elliott's shirt and unbuttoned it, exposing the entrance wound. It was not large, but blood seeped from it. Joaquin pulled the shirt up from Elliott's back to view the exit wound. He grimaced at the larger hole and the blood flow. The bullet had entered his right side above the belt. *I hope it didn't hit anything important.* As he reached for his handkerchief he said softly, "I need to bind this up proper. Are there any sheets or anything in the cabin to use for bandaging?"

"I reckon there's something thet'll do in there. You go on ahead, boy. I'll keep an eyeball peeled on Chacon." Chacon lay back on his left side, moaning.

Joaquin entered the small cabin through the bullet-riddled door and saw one man lying dead, sprawled out on his back, blood pooling under him. The other dead man was crumpled in the far corner of the room. Joaquin walked into the back room that served as a bedroom for Chacon. Visually sweeping the room, he observed the broken window and the dead woman lying on the bed. She had been shot twice, once through the heart and once in the forehead. The revolver she had been holding lay next to her outstretched hand.

Joaquin reached down, closed the woman's eyes, picked up the revolver and stuck it in his gun belt. Then he gathered up bandaging material and returned to where Elliott leaned against the boulder watching Chacon.

Chapo Carter had just arrived. "Joe Butler's dead, Elliott. I'm sorry. He took a round through his throat when we rushed the other cabin. Carlos was shot through the calf of his leg, but he's goin' to be alright—jest hurtin' bad is all an' can't ride."

Oh, my God. Joe dead? Joaquin stood wide-eyed, holding the bandage material.

Elliott closed his eyes, sighed. "How about Shaw?"

"Thet Kansas boy done good. Nary a scratch ... 'ceptin' fer them blisters on his feet." Carter turned and gestured back beyond the cabins. "He's guardin' a prisoner at the cave yonder an' takin' care of Carlos, I reckon."

"Only one prisoner?"

"Yup, jest one an' he's got one o' his thumbs shot off. All them others wanted to shoot it out—they're all dead."

"The women? ..."

"Dead." Carter reached in his shirt pocket and brought out his tobacco and papers. He built himself and Elliott cigarettes, lit both, handed one to Elliott, and exhaled slowly. "Them women was meaner fighters than the men. It was one o' 'em thet got Butler when he went in."

"All of 'em ... *dead?*" asked Joaquin. His lips were dry. He had trouble swallowing—his mouth tasted like cotton.

"All dead, son." Carter watched Joaquin plug Elliott's bullet wounds and bind them securely. Joaquin then he moved over to Chacon and bandaged his shoulder wound.

Elliott took a drag from his cigarette. "With several of us all shot up, I reckon we'll stay here till we kin all ride outta here. Chapo, you check the corral o'er yonder an' see what brands are on them cows. Then you kin help us bury these bodies and clean up the cabins." He paused, peering out across the mountains. "Bury Joe inside the cave. I don't give a damn where them others gits laid. We'll use one cabin fer sleepin' an' restin' up—the other fer Chacon an' the other prisoner."

He ground out the cigarette under his boot. "Joaquin, you go on to the cave, help bandage up Carlos an' thet Mexican prisoner. Then come on back with 'em."

"Sure you'll be okay?" Joaquin did not like the paleness

he saw in Elliott's face.

"I'm fit as a fiddle, *mijo*. You go on, ya hear."

Elliott watched the Rangers head off in two different directions. He walked over to Chacon and looked down at the bandit. *Not long ago, I woulda killed ya for what ya done to Lou.* "This here day's been a long time comin'. Afore you're done, you'll wish thet boy'd shot you dead. You're goin' back, standin' trial, an' then I figger you'll swing from the gallows fer what you've done."

Elliott reached down, grabbed the outlaw's good arm and helped him to his feet. They started walking toward the cabin. Turning to the outlaw, he drawled, "Oh yeah, Chacon. I plumb forgot. It's mah sworn duty to advise ya thet I have an arrest warrant fer your *low-down* murdererin' hide." They reached the porch of the cabin. *I'm shore proud o' the boy—hell, I done fair myself today.*

CHAPTER TWENTY-SEVEN

I t was early October when the four Arizona Rangers rode back into the United States and the town of Douglas from Mexico. They had been gone for more than a month. As Viento trotted along, Elliott thought it was good to be back. He was tired of the travel, the stress of watching Chacon—day in and day out. His gunshot wound still hurt especially with the horseback riding, even though he knew it must be about healed. *Damned lucky there wasn't no infection.*

Days earlier, Elliott had telegraphed Captain Rynnning at headquarters with a short message from Mexico advising the Rangers had Indio Chacon in custody and that Ranger Joe Butler had been killed in the line of duty.

On their way back with Indio Chacon and the other rustler, Colonel Kosterlitzky had met them in Fronteras, Sonora with bad news. Their former comrade Bill Wade had somehow overpowered the two Rurales, killing both of them as they were transporting him back to the United States. At first, Elliott couldn't believe it, but then he remembered the man had been deadly back in the old days. One of the Rurales let their guard down, and Wade had been waiting to act. Kosterlitzky and all of his Rurales were out scouring the countryside trying to locate Wade. They feared that he had gotten back across the border and was no longer in Mexico.

The Colonel had insisted on taking custody of the other rustler captured with Chacon. He pointed out to the

Americans that they did not have an arrest warrant for him as they had for Chacon. Elliott argued for keeping the man in his custody, but in the end Kosterlitzky won out. Carlos, the Rurale who had assisted them in capturing Chacon, had remained behind with Kosterlitsky in Mexico. As the Rangers rode out of Fronteras, Mexico heading for Agua Prieta with Chacon as their prize, Elliott wondered just how long the rustler left behind might live. He'd thought his life wasn't worth a damned plugged nickel.

At Ranger Headquarters, Captain Rynning and Lieutenant Wheeler stood on the front porch waiting for them. The Rangers rode up to the corral, dismounted, and tied their horses and pack mules to the hitch rack at the corral. Since Chacon's hands were tied behind his back, Joaquin helped him dismount from his horse.

Captain Rynning, followed by Harry Wheeler, strode up to the group near the corral. He smiled as he looked at the worn out Rangers, their haggard faces with several days' growth of beard. "I'm damned proud of each of you men." He paused and frowned. "I'm so sorry about Joe. Harry got word to his family."

Elliott shuffled his feet. "We buried 'im in the cave down there, Tom. It was the best we could do. We covered the grave with heavy rocks an' said a few words."

"I'm sure you boys did everything you could for him." Rynning turned to Wheeler. "Harry, would you transport Chacon over to the jail? I'd like to have a word with Elliott and Joaquin."

"Sure will, Tom." Wheeler walked over to the bandit, replaced the rope around his wrists with handcuffs. Then he peered at Chapo Carter and Frank Shaw. "You two mind helping me get Chacon over to the jail?" He smiled at Carter and Shaw. "Once we get him locked up, I'll buy both of you the biggest steak in town. What do you say to that offer?"

Carter answered for both of them. "Let's get movin', Harry. I'm plumb starved."

Rynning ushered Elliott and Joaquin inside the Ranger office. Joaquin felt a knot in the pit of his stomach. *A private meeting? Why?*

Elliott rubbed his right knee. "What's goin' on Tom? Is there a problem with them Rurales on account o' Bill?" Not waiting for an answer, he added, "Hell, I'd never guessed thet Wade was man 'nough to take Arturo ... much less both o' them Rurales."

"No one's blaming you, Elliott. I'd have sent him back, too." Rynning bit his lower lip. "Something else has come up, and I'm not sure how to tell you ..."

"Hell, jest say it, Tom. An' quit lollygaggin'," said Elliott.

"Joaquin, it's about your friend—Carmen Ponce."

"What 'bout her? Elliott interrupted.

Startled, Joaquin frowned. "Yeah, what about Carmen?"

Rynning said softly, "She's been hurt Joaquin ... hurt bad."

"*Hurt!*" Joaquin's heart pounded. "What happened?"

"It was Wade. He beat her almost to death and ..."

"*What?*" Elliott and Joaquin answered in unison. Joaquin's mouth dropped. His stomach was queasy.

Elliott stepped toward Rynning, his voice hard, "What in the *hell* are ya talkin' 'bout?"

"Both of you ... just calm down, and I'll tell you what I know." Rynning continued, "I ... I'm sorry Joaquin. He ... after he beat her, well he ... he raped her. I'm so sorry."

Stunned, Joaquin finally managed to stammer, "*Oh, my God!*" He covered his face with his hands. He swallowed hard several times then closed his eyes trying not to envision the terrible wrong to his best, good friend. He tried to speak. Tears streamed down his cheeks. "Why? Why would he *do* that?" He choked. "How's Carmen? Where is she?"

"Easy now, boy. She was hurt bad, but she's doing better now." Rynning placed his arm around Joaquin's shoulders. "She's with her father out at the ranch."

Elliott spoke with a hard metallic ring in his voice, "Where's Wade? Any idée?"

"None. He told Carmen he wanted Joaquin to know it was him."

"The *sumbitch!*" Joaquin slammed his fist on the desk. "I shoulda killed him down in Mexico, Elliott. I ..." A sob broke his voice. He took a deep breath, trying to control himself.

Elliott patted his back. "Ain't your fault, *mijo*. None o' us coulda figgered on this hyar devilry."

Rynning took Joaquin by the shoulders, "Look, Joaquin ... take some time off—whatever you need. Go to the ranch and take care of Carmen. We'll find Wade and bring him in."

Elliott's eyes were hard, his jaw clenched. "He's right, Joaquin. She needs you now more'n ever. You go on ... an' take good care o' her."

Joaquin did not wait for any further instructions. He sprinted out the door to his paint horse. With fumbling fingers, he untied the horse, swung up into the saddle in one fluid motion, and touched his spurs to an animal that was worn out from the long ride from Mexico.

Shaking his head, Elliott stared off into the distance and sighed deeply. "My Gawd, Tom. One o' our own doin' this hyar dirty work."

"I know it. It's bad enough for us, but that little gal. I feel so bad for her."

"I'll find 'im ... no matter how long it takes. I reckon I'll put Viento up an' them pack mules then maybe I'll git some grub myself." Elliott started out the door, hesitating on the threshold, "Tom, you git any leads on Bill's whereabouts, you let me know. Ya hear?"

"You'll be the first to know."

"*Gracias.*" Elliott's spurs clinked musically on the wooden floor as he strode out.

Elliott was unsaddling the last pack mule when he heard someone approaching the corral behind him. He turned. A Mexican boy around ten years old stood without speaking, his hands fidgeting.

Impatiently, Elliott motioned for the boy to come closer. "*¡Venga aqui! No tenga miedo.*"

The young boy stood firm where he was, not moving then took a step closer.

"*¿Donde esta, Señor Joaquin Campbell?*" asked the boy.

"*No está aqui. ¿Quien quiere saber?*"

"A man ... he wants thees *papel* geev to heem." The boy held up a piece of folded paper.

Elliott took it from him and ripped it open. He read the paper then read it again. His jaw tightened, his mouth twisted in rage. Frightened, the boy stepped back and turned to run. Elliott reached out and patted the boy on the head as he tucked the message into his shirt pocket below the silver five-pointed badge.

"*Yo se lo doy a Joaquin. Gracias.*" He smiled down at the boy, "*Digale que usted le dio el papel a Joaquin ... no a mi. ¿Comprende?*"

Elliott reached in his pants pocket and tossed a quarter to the boy. The boy deftly caught the coin and smiled up at his latest benefactor.

"*Sí, Señor.* I weel tell heem I geev to *Señor Joaquin.*" The boy turned and walked back toward Sixth Street.

CHAPTER TWENTY-EIGHT

J oaquin spurred his paint horse faster, the wind blowing his hot tears dry. *Carmen ... oh my God, Carmen. Why wasn't I there for you?* The horse was lathered up and so fatigued that Joaquin honestly didn't believe they would make it until he saw the ranch buildings in front of him. He rode into the yard and leaped from his horse leaving the reins grounded. Stumbling up onto the porch, he burst into the house.

His mother turned sharply from the kitchen stove. "Joaquin!"

"Mom!"

They embraced, holding each other tightly.

"How is she, Mom?"

"As well as can be expected, I reckon. She's been askin' fer ya. I told her you was still down in Mexico last I heerd an' thet you'd be along as soon as ya got back."

"We heard about it when we rode into Douglas the day before yesterday. I rode hard as I could in getting here." Joaquin's eyes begged the question.

"She's up on the north end of Cienega Creek with her father. You can take my sorrel, son. Your horse most likely is plumb wore out." Marian Campbell fussed with her apron. "Leave your paint horse tied up in the barn. I'll curry 'im down good 'afore I turn 'im out to eat and drink. Supper'll be ready when you'all git back this evening."

"Thanks, Mom."

Marian took her son's head in her hands and brought it

toward her. Planting a loving kiss on his forehead, she said, "You go on now."

Joaquin turned and walked out to his lathered horse, his spurs clinking on the wooden porch. As he gathered the reins in his hands and walked his pony toward the barn, he said, "I'm sorry I rode you so hard, paint horse, but it had to be done for Carmie—you understand, don't you, boy?"

He found them on the upper north end of Cienega Creek. Domingo and Carmen sat on the ground, working hard at pulling a calf from its mother's womb. No head showed. A breech birth.

Domingo had placed a cotton rope on the calf's legs and he and Carmen were pulling hard, trying to get the calf out as quickly as possible. Joaquin moved in quickly next to Carmen, dug his heels in, and pulled with all his might. The calf began emerging, slowly at first and then suddenly, out it popped. All three rescuers fell backwards, the calf landing on top of them. Domingo quickly cleared the mucous from its mouth as Carmen attempted to hold the slick heifer calf.

"Well, I reckon you folks are sure lucky, what with me coming along when I did to give ya a hand," Joaquin joked.

Standing, the three looked at each other's wet, dirty clothing. A chuckle rose from Joaquin's throat. Domingo grinned then Carmen giggled, and they laughed together till tears flowed.

Carmen finally recovered enough to help the calf stand near its mother. The little calf wobbled from side to side barely able to stand, but appeared to be breathing with little difficulty.

Carmen smiled at Joaquin. "I'm so glad you're here, Joaquin."

Before he could answer, her father stepped forward, extending his hand, *"Bien venido, Joaquin."* The handshake extended into a heartfelt embrace.

"Gracias, Domingo."

Carmen turned toward her father, *"Papá*, Joaquin and I need some time to talk ... alone. Do you mind?"

"No, mi'ja. Allá los espero." Domingo took one last look at the cow and calf. The cow was now standing, the calf having enjoyed its first meal of fresh milk. He turned, mounted his horse, and rode down Cienega Creek toward the ranch.

Joaquin and Carmen rode farther up the creek to the old swimming hole and they tied their horses to mesquite trees in the riparian area. Joaquin followed Carmen to their favorite spot in a small grove of cottonwood trees. They had spent many happy hours laughing in the shade of those trees, enjoying the cold water in the scorching hot summers and the peace and solitude of the cool, windy falls. It was "their place" —past, present, and future. And so, on that day in the fall of 1904, it seemed natural to go there.

Carmen stood near the water's edge. The cool breeze rustled the few remaining leaves and worked at disturbing her beautiful black hair braided into two separate braids hanging down her shoulders.

Joaquin walked up behind her and gently encircled her with his arms, pulling her to him. He smelled her fragrant hair as he hugged her close and whispered, "Carmen ... I ... love you so."

She turned to face him, and he could see her eyes welling up with tears; there was still some swelling and bruising around her eyes, nose and mouth. It angered him to think of what had happened to her. *"That son-of-a-bitch. I'll kill 'im!"*

Carmen hugged him then placed her head on his chest struggling to talk through the sobs in her chest, she said, "He hates you so much Joaquin, but he hates me more because I'm Mexican."

"I'll find him. I *swear* it."

She hugged him again and sat down near the water. "Joaquin, I honestly do not understand how some people can hate and hurt others for the color of their skin or where they come from."

"Carmen, I ... I'm so sorry I wasn't there for you." Joaquin reached out and took her hand, holding it gently, his own eyes welling up with tears.

"You musn't blame yourself. It ... just happened ... that's all. And I have to move on. But I'll never be able to forget ... *never!*

He listened quietly as she told him everything that happened to her that terrible day. He knew she desperately needed to tell someone, that it was good for her to talk about the incident. As Joaquin listened, he couldn't keep tears from trickling down his face or control the trembling rage that burned deep within him. He waited until she finished speaking. Finally, she gazed down into the water, saying nothing.

"Carmen, you're my best good friend—the only one I'll ever have in my time in the sun." He moved closer to her and put his arm over her shoulders. He wiped at the tears on his face, swallowing hard. "I've loved you all my life, and I know you love me, too. I will always be there for you. I want to be your husband, the father of our children, and most of all, I want you to be my friend forever."

She smiled, turning sad eyes to Joaquin. "Forever is a long time, my friend."

"Carmen, these past months I've found that life is hard—some times brutal. You and I have lived sheltered lives here on the ranch. I ... I had to kill some men in Morenci. One of them was trying to hurt Elliott. I shot him, Carmen."

Joaquin looked out over the water. "Anyhow, I felt bad for it; even though I know it had to be done."

"It's natural to feel bad about taking a life, Joaquin. That's why I don't want you to go after Wade. Let the Rangers or other peace officers arrest him. You're too personally involved in this." Carmen pursed her lips. "Promise me you won't go after him." When he hesitated, she reached out and grasped his hands, pleading with him, *"Promise me!"*

He hugged her tightly, not wanting to let her go. "I promise, Carmen. You have my word on it." He released her. "Will you marry me at the end of my enlistment?"

"Joaquin, I ... I don't know if it's a good thing for us to marry. I love you very much, but ..."

"There's no but, Carmen. I love you, too. That's all that matters."

"I wish it were that simple, my love. This world that we live in may not be ready to accept a mixed marriage. I don't want you hurt."

Joaquin pleaded, "We'll make it work. *I know it!*"

Carmen held his hands. "No promises, my friend, but I hope you realize that I love you dearly ... more than anyone. I have truly loved you since I was a little girl."

She walked back to the water's edge. "I'll have an answer for you when your enlistment is up. Can you allow me that time to think things through?"

Not satisfied with her answer, Joaquin hesitated. He bit at his lower lip. "I'll wait for your answer, Carmen. It's the least I can do considering all that's happened to you."

She grimaced. "I may have a baby from that monster. Can you live with that?

"Are you sure?"

"No ... but it's very possible." She began to cry. Joaquin walked toward her, but she stepped back from him, waiting for his answer.

"Carmen, it doesn't matter. We'll take care of the baby just like one of our own."

He straightened up and took a deep breath. "Don't let anyone take our life together away from us, especially folks who hate others for the color of their skin. Please don't allow them to decide for us." He let his words sink in. "That's about all I have to say ... except ... *Te amo, mi querida.*"

She turned, walked to him and held him tightly with her head against his chest. She murmured softly, "I love you, too."

As they stood frozen in time on the banks of Cienega Creek, a mourning dove called out in the cool fall air. Decadent cottonwood leaves parted reluctantly from their branches, suddenly dropping and were hesitantly carried to distant locations by the billowing wind and the cool waters of the creek.

CHAPTER TWENTY-NINE

At dusk Elliott saddled Viento, and by the time he rode to Sixth Street, it was almost pitch black with no moon to illuminate the way. His purpose was clear. He pulled Viento up in front of the Cowboy Home Place Saloon. He didn't tie the horse to the hitch rack as others had done that evening, but dismounted close to the boardwalk with the reins left hanging.

Elliott stepped up onto the board sidewalk. His spurs jingled as he strode to the batwing doors, the fringes on the sides of his leather-riding chaps rustled in the breeze. He placed his hands on the doors, peering into the murky interior of the saloon. The coal-oil lamps dimly lit the room that was filled to capacity with rowdy customers. Smoke had drifted to the ceiling of the room and hung there, providing an eerie and ominous feeling to the setting.

Two bartenders stood behind the bar to his left, but the fat one at the far end near the wall did not appear to be serving customers. *Thet's odd now, ain't it?* Elliott scanned the room, hesitating at a familiar figure. Bill Wade sat at a table in the rear of the room, facing the doorway. Elliott quickly scanned the rest of the barroom.

Elliott stepped inside the loud, smoke-filled room, ignoring the men lined up at the bar. The batwing doors flopped behind him. Wade stood and moved to his left. Elliott paused to assess the situation. *Don't like it 'atall.* To face Wade, he now stood in the center of the room with his back to the bar.

Elliott cocked his head toward the bartender near the

wall. "*You...fat man*! Put your hands up on the bar away from thet shotgun. *Now!*"

The boisterous, loud room transformed into a quiet stillness. The fat bartender reluctantly placed both hands up on the bar. Elliott turned toward Wade to face him about twenty feet away. He stepped slightly to his right to see any peripheral movement behind him at the bar.

"Where's Joaquin?" Wade's contemptuous words hung in the air.

"Don't reckon he'll be joinin'us, Bill."

"I don't have nothin 'agin you, Elliott. It's the greaser lover boy I want. You walk outta here an' you won't git hurt."

A smile toyed at Elliott's face then disappeared. "I'm plumb surprised ya ain't figgered out thet ya don't always git what ya want in life. Your bullyin' an' killin' days are over." His glare bored into Wade.

"We go back a long ways, Elliott ... rangerin' an' them gunfightin' days." Wade's eyes wavered as he spoke.

"The ol' ways an' them gunfightin' days is long gone ... an' you crossed over the line." Elliott's voice had a metallic ring to it.

Wade's face twitched. "Don't make me *kill ya*! You was fast in the ol' days, but I always said thet I could take ya even then—if'n I wanted to. Now, *look at ya*! Hell, ya ain't nothin' but an ol' man."

"I reckon I am a tad older ... happens as ya move along in life." Elliott kept his voice soft. He stood relaxed, his right arm hanging next to the old pistol belt and holster, the worn brown pistol butt halfway between his elbow and wrist. "But you, Wade—you're nothin' but a yeller, *low-down* dog."

The sharp words hung in the air and for a few seconds it seemed as though time stood still. Then the empty quietness of the room broke in the deadly swiftness of both men. Their guns exploded almost simultaneously, belching flame and lead into the dimly lit, smoke-filled saloon.

A bewildered look came over Wade's face as he looked down at his right shoulder. Wade's gaze continued on below the shoulder where his arm should have been. Elliott's heavy .45 caliber bullet had nearly severed his right arm below the shoulder. Blood dripped from the wound. Wade screamed, reaching with his left hand for another pistol tucked into his belt.

Elliott bent slightly at the knees, pulled the trigger back on his revolver, then fanned the hammer back with the heel of his left hand ... once ... twice ... three times. The heavy slugs tore into Wade's chest flinging him backwards onto the table behind him, and over it onto the saloon floor.

Smoke swirled from the end of Elliott's gun barrel. He reloaded as he peered soberly down at the dead Ranger—a man who had been his fellow peace officer once. A man who had stood for law and order but then for whatever reasons had tarnished the badge forever. He sighed deeply and spoke softly. "Thet's fer 'lil Carmen ... I reckon."

The old gunman spun the revolver expertly on his index finger, forward ... three times, then backward three times, with the heavy revolver seating itself smoothly by its own weight into the weathered holster. As he turned toward the bar, a loud shotgun blast ripped through the room. BLAM! *The bartender!* Someone to his left yelped out in pain. The blast—like searing embers—lifted Elliott off his feet and hurled him onto the floor. He clawed for his six-shooter, but couldn't grip it. The room swirled around ... and around.

Footsteps approached. Someone shouted. Then shots ... two? A body hit the floor nearby. Was he dreaming? *How long ...have I been here?* The floor—so hard—so cold. So weak. He lay there knowing he should get up, but he couldn't. *I ... can't ... reach mah rosary. Wel-l-l ...*

His young wife stood over him, holding their son in one arm. Her free arm outstretched toward him, urgently reaching out to him.

"Ven, mi amor," she whispered, smiling at him.

He reached out to her, briefly touching her hand. *Let's ... go on home, Maria. I reckon it's been way too long at thet.* Suddenly, he didn't feel cold anymore. It seemed as though he was in a warm cozy room with the wood stove plumb cranked up in the dead of winter. He felt a peace he had never known before. *Like sittin' on the riverbank on a fine sunny day.*

Then just as quickly as they had appeared, his wife and son's images slowly faded away and darkness overcame Elliott.

CHAPTER THIRTY
Fall, 1904

I t was a day not unlike many other fall days along the San Pedro River. The large cottonwood trees displayed their naked branches with a few lingering golden leaves swirling in the soft winds blowing down the valley floor. Joaquin held Carmen close to him as they gazed down at the two graves on a small knoll a hundred yards or so from Elliott's ranch house. Fresh flowers decorated the wooden crosses of both graves, and there were no weeds visible. Hao Li was undoubtedly responsible for the excellent care.

"Mistah Hoe-kin. You come please." The words startled them. They turned toward the ranch house and saw Hao Li on the porch motioning them to come to the house. Joaquin and Carmen walked back, holding hands.

They stepped up on the small porch and heard an old familiar voice. "You two lollygaggin' agin? Food's gittin' cold, young 'uns." Joaquin thought again of the two graves, *Maria and the first Joaquin ... Elliott would never allow them to be forgotten.*

Joaquin grinned at Elliott sitting in the old homemade rocking chair on the porch. Megan Campbell stood behind the old Ranger, rubbing his shoulders. Timmy Campbell sat on the porch next to Elliott, his crutches lying nearby.

Elliott had been on the mend for about a month since the shooting, his left arm bandaged and in a sling. The shotgun blast had also injured his left hip and leg, but he was expected to fully recover the use of his arm and leg over time. Luckily for him, a bystander had taken the brunt of the blast from the shotgun the fat bartender had wielded. Before he could shoot Elliott again, Chapo Carter had entered the saloon and shot him dead.

"Mistah Hoe-kin, you and Miss Ca-min, come in, sit down—eat, please." The Chinese man motioned them to come inside and sit at the table.

Elliott looked up at Megan. "Ahh ... Megan darlin', you are the *finest* woman thet I've ever knowed."

She smiled down at him without speaking.

Elliott continued, "You two heerd 'bout Chacon?"

"I heard his trial in Tucson was about over," answered Joaquin.

"Over fer shore an' he was found guilty o' murderin' your dad, ol' man Williams, and his cowpuncher. The judge sentenced him to hang next month. Ole JLB is plumb tickled. You reckon on goin' up to watch?"

Joaquin thought as Hao Li paced nervously inside the ranch house waiting for them. "No ... I reckon not, Elliott. I've seen too much killing for my taste lately. I'm glad he has to answer for what he did though—mighty glad the law worked in bringing him to justice."

"I done told ya it would, now didn't I?" teased the old Ranger.

Joaquin nodded and smiled.

Elliott cleared his throat. "I ... uh ... we ... wanted both of ya to know. Meg and I figger on gittin' married next month."

"Well, that's great news!" Joaquin slapped his leg.

"Congratulations!" Carmen gave Elliott and Megan each a hug. "I wish you both the very best."

"Thank ya, *mija*. What 'bout you two?"

"We're still ... thinking on the matter, Elliott." Carmen smiled at him then looked down at the floor.

Elliott's blue eyes twinkled. "Wel-l-l ... you'll make the right choice, Carmen ... when the time comes, I reckon."

Megan spoke up. "Carmen, I sent in certification of your education to the college in Tucson along with your application. We'll just have to wait and see if they'll accept you."

"Thank you, Meg. I truly appreciate all that you've done for me."

"*No es nada*. We're in dire need of good teachers."

Elliott chimed in, "Carmen, I spoke to Captain Rynning. He said he'd talk to the Governor. I reckon he's got some clout with them college fellers."

"I hope it won't be too much trouble for him?" asked Carmen.

"Naw ... I reckon not," returned Elliott.

Elliott turned toward Joaquin. "In the mean time, the Rangers got work to do, *mi'jo*. I heerd thet one o' the banks in Tucson was held up jest last week. Them robbers was usin' one o' them new fangled ... horseless carriages. They got plumb away from town—*pronto* accordin' to Harry."

He looked down at his bandaged arm and sighed. "I jest don't know what the hell the world's comin' to, boy. It shore is changin' fast fer this ol' man." Elliott looked out over the southwestern landscape from the little porch. "I'm thinkin' o' hangin' up mah guns when the enlistment is up, *mi'jo*."

"*No!* Not you, Elliott."

"Maybe. I figger on spendin' as much time with Meg an' Timmy as I kin; maybe I'll git this here ranch up an' runnin'—like in the ol' days."

"The Rangers won't ever be the same without you, Elliott."

"I reckon all you boys'll do jest fine, Joaquin." Elliott smiled broadly.

Joaquin looked fondly at the older man. There would be tough, dangerous times in the months ahead as an Arizona

Ranger. "I've sure learned a lot from you and the others."

"You're gittin' there, boy."

Joaquin felt he was becoming a better lawman, but he also knew that he had a long way to go. "Do you think they'll keep the Rangers?"

Elliott rubbed his chin. "I reckon fer a few years anyhow ... least ways till them Democrats take over the legislature." He rubbed his right knee. "Good lawmen will always be needed in Arizona, *mijo*. Hell, 'pecially if'n we become a state."

Megan spoke up, "I heard the powers that be in the territory are pushing hard to include Arizona in the union."

"That's so—ol' Teddy Roosevelt wants to make New Mexico and Arizona Territories into one *big* state," reflected the old Ranger. "It don't make no never mind to me." He stretched his bad arm. "You youngun's best git in the house afore Li comes after you with a butcher knife."

As Joaquin turned to go inside, he thought about what had been nagging him and keeping him awake nights. Would Carmen decide to marry him? He gazed at her longingly then smiled to himself. He would make sure of that— no matter what.

Elliott heard the screen door shut as Hao Li ushered the young couple into the small ranch house. He eased back in the rocking chair, feeling Megan's strong hands massaging his shoulders and reached back with his good hand to pat hers.

He thought of the times long ago when he was a young cowpuncher ridin' hard in the rain and lightnin' turnin' the stampeded herd out on the lonely Texas plains, fightin' Injuns with a vengeance thet was plumb wrong an' them Spaniards with a clear purpose thet was plumb right. He recalled the gunfights ... the deaths ... too many—way too many.

He closed his eyes. Age was kinda like a thief in the night—one day you was young doin' anything thet pleased ya—the next day, your step jest didn't have the spring it once had an' in the mornin' you was stove up and gimpy. You was still a helluva man, but older and feelin' it.

He figgered he'd mulled his past long enough, his future had sneaked up on 'im faster than he cared to think about. The Old West he had come to know an' love was plumb gone and the only thing thet was fer shore in his future was Megan.

Let them young Rangers chase down the Tucson bank robbers who had jest gotten away in one o' them new-fangled horseless ... whatever the hell they was called.

Elliott broke off his thoughts and looked over at Tim who sat quietly on the porch next to him.

"Timmy ... mah good friend ... you reckon ya could walk with this ol' man down by the crick, boy?" Not waiting for an answer, he stood. "Might need some help. And I shore need a friend—not jest any, mind ya, but a goodun'—like you, *mi'jo.*"

The young boy smiled and eagerly gathered up his wooden crutches. "Yes sir. I'd like that ... Dad."

THE END

Printed in the United States
206891BV00002B/29/A

9 781583 852392